BRYHER

THE

Fourteenth of October

A NOVEL

PANTHEON BOOKS

NEW YORK

FOR

𝔚. 𝔖.

i

IT WAS OCTOBER. The leaves were gold above my head; single ones fluttered from a bough as if waiting for some archer to shoot them down to their fellows. I crept as quietly as I could from bush to bush, trying to make no noise. At any moment I expected to hear Leofwen's voice, "Where are you, Wulf, come back to me." But I must be a mile already from our farm, and once I got to the edge of the wood the ford would be below me and I could climb a tree and watch the battle.

I was not frightened, but I jumped every time that a wood rat rustled through the russet litter underfoot. There had been something in the air for days; nobody could settle to his task; the women had been irritable, and a calf had died for no apparent reason. Then a messenger had galloped into our yard, at the very end of a peaceful Sunday afternoon, calling out as soon as he could see us, "The Danes, the Danes. . . ."

There had been no peace as long as I could remember. We never knew where the shield-hung dragon-ships would strike. Every spring, as the corn was sowed, we wondered whether we should reap it. If a stone were dislodged from a wall, the shepherds would not mend it before the raiding season was over; then it would be winter and too late. The whole eastern coast was sinking back into wilderness. "When I was a boy, there were twenty great farms between here and York," my father had told me grimly; "now there are three." Even when we drove the raiders away, herders were killed or survivors drifted inland, cattle were lost or sold for ransom money, the heather crept back to the fields and isolated us, no more corn was planted.

There were rumours that our neighbor, Egbert, had bought protection from the Danes. He so seldom took his turn at watching the cliffs. The burden of our defence had fallen upon my father. Nobody had any time for me. Since my mother's death, and I had been so young then that I could hardly remember her, my father always seemed to be in the lookout up the hill, or working in his fields. "Master Rodwen has done more for us than any man in Yorkshire," the women said gratefully when they came to help with the hay.

I do not know what would have become of me if it had not been for Leofwen. He was too old to work with the herds; besides, he was a harper, though now the thanes were too poor to pay him for his songs. He did odd jobs about the yard, and while he was mending straps or helping me feed the chickens he told me stories of the great, golden days when people were happy, before there were raids. "In those days the Earls were men," he would add as we sat together on the stone bench under the wall. He did not have to tell me about our rulers. We all knew that Edwin and Morkere would not defend us, no matter how often we petitioned them for even a score of heavy-armed soldiers to fill up the gaps in our ranks.

Leofwen had forbidden me to leave the courtyard, but it was more than mere curiosity that had sent me out to the wood. I had to be there; an obscure feeling had been driving me towards the river all morning. Something was going to happen. I supposed it was victory, and in a way I could not explain I had to be part of it. I pushed a branch aside gently, crawled over the roots of a great oak and came to a clearing where I had often sat to watch the birds. Beyond me the moors stretched in bare ridges out towards the cliffs.

There were the Danes, moving down the bare slope of the opposite hill. There must have been sixty of them, three at least to every one of us Saxons. They were fresh from feasting on our cattle. I could almost hear them laughing. A straggler was tossing a dart into the air and catching it as it fell. "Let a Dane be sure his axe is sharp; nothing else will trouble him," had always been my father's bitter comment; and now that their leader strode forward, holding his great shield so that all I could see was the helmet crest above it, I knew how true this saying was. The horsehair falling over the rim as if it were a beak, the power, the ruthlessness of his movements, made him seem less a man than a gigantic bird of prey. His followers were like him. They had no wives trembling in the villages behind them; the smoke that rose was not from their barns. Even if our line was strong enough to hold them, they could break off the fight and retreat to their ship, to come back and plunder us again the following year.

"When Danish boys are twelve, they think only of their weapons," Leofwen had reproved me earlier that summer when I had run away from a bow and arrow practice to look for frogs along our pond. "Must we always think of war?" I had sighed; for a great, green grasshopper had hopped over my fingers, and I had heard a little hawk in the reeds. "Yes, we must; the Danes have men coming to them from the north and the east, and we get fewer every season." "Then why do we fight at all?" I had grumbled, for I did not want to go back to the bare common where the older boys laughed at the weakness of our shots. "Because it is natural for a man to defend his home," Leofwen had reproved me, taking me angrily by the arm and marching me back to the butts.

The Danes were almost at the ford before they saw our men. They drew together in a moment, closed their ranks and shouted. It was the first time that I had heard their famous battle cry; it rose regularly into the air with an ominous pause between each beat, the terrifying way that rocks crack and then topple into the sea. I pushed out of my hiding place and into the open. Up to this instant everything had been vague fear; I had never doubted our victory. Now the solid group of dark bucklers, their reserves behind them, moved against my father's men strung in a single line along our side of the river. Egbert had never reached them. There were no reinforcements. "I did not know that it was going to be like this," I heard myself muttering. A few arrows hummed through the air; the black vulture-like band moved steadily and slowly forward. I watched a man drop into the stream; I saw our crest; the axes swung suddenly. I closed my eyes. I could not breathe, an ice wall seemed to close over me. We have to win, I thought; this is so unjust, why doesn't Egbert come? Let it be over, I was praying, let everything be right again. Then the shouts lessened, and I looked in front of me. It was over, everything was over. The Danes were climbing the hill, and where our men had waited there was no banner, only a couple of raiders stripping armour from a dozen dead bodies. I shrieked; an arrow whizzed past my ear and stuck in the next tree. A Dane pointed towards me and I turned and ran, trembling, sobbing, with the branches smacking my face, towards our village.

I had gone straight up to the old barn and lay looking at the rafters. An occasional mouse scuffled through the straw. The women had looked at me curiously but had not tried to stop me. I wondered at first where Leofwen was; then I remembered that he had probably gone with the elders to intercede with the Danes. They would take our cattle, probably they would fire the crops. Perhaps we should have to take to the moors and beg as I had seen so many do in the few short years I had been alive. I did not care. I wanted to leave this terrible spot, never to be reminded of it. I kept seeing my father's face, his smile as he had lifted me up, in babyhood, to see the horses. The hours passed and it grew dark; I heard feet trampling the stones, and knew without being told that they had brought his body back to the courtyard. I shivered, I pressed my face into the straw, trying not to see the axes. Then I must have slept, for it was night when Leofwen shook me gently. "Wake up, Wulf," he whispered, his big hand on my shoulder, "wake up, I have to talk to you."

Leofwen's cloak swung open, and I saw that he had a horn lantern under it. He leaned down to clear a place on the boards and I noticed a great mark, as if a stick had struck him, across his cheek. I stared in surprise for I had not known that he had been wounded. "Egbert," he said grimly, as he caught my eyes.

"Listen, Wulf," he went on, and though I had seen

terrible things during the past day and night, none of them had frightened me as much as his face did now. It was full of sorrow, of the sorrow they say that Othin felt when he foresaw Ragnerok. "You are my foster son, now that your father is dead—even my son. I hoped . . ." He could say nothing more and I flung my arms round his neck. "Don't leave me," I begged, for I feared that he was desperately wounded. "You cannot leave me too."

"Quiet," he managed to stammer, "quiet. Egbert gave me this," and he touched his cheek, "so that I should not come to find you."

"Why?" Egbert had always hated my father. "It's easy to be just with a rich farm," he had often jeered, but Leofwen was now my guardian.

"The Danes have demanded hostages."

I nodded. It was part of their usual plan to strip the coast of defenders. But Egbert had no son, and his nephew was safely with the Earls.

"Egbert suggested your name to the elders."

"Suggested me?" I looked up in surprise. Such a possibility had never entered my head. By tradition the only boy of a man fallen in battle was exempt, unless, perhaps, it were an Earl's son, taken not for a village but a kingdom.

"There are two ways open, Wulf, and you must consider both carefully because I cannot choose for you. I protested at the meeting that it was against the law and that you were too young. I was overruled. They say that there are no other youths left in this neighbourhood, and that is true."

I shifted a little in the straw and clutched Leofwen's hand. "But why does Egbert want to be rid of me?" I asked. I was humble now; yesterday had taught me I had no power as yet to lift the great axes.

"He wants the thaneship, and that he will get because he is the only man of fighting age left for twenty miles. Only as you come to your strength and your land he sees a rival in you, both to his nephew and himself. He hated your father, and you are too like . . . Rodwen."

"That is all I have left to me," I said.

Leofwen nodded, and we sat in silence for a couple of minutes. The tallow was burning down and I was shivering, though Leofwen had his arm about me and his cloak.

"If you are willing to go as hostage," he said at last, "you will leave tomorrow morning. You are young to go among strangers. Yet your lands will be under the joint protection of all the thanes until you return to claim them, and not even Egbert will dare take them from you. You will be trained as a soldier, and perhaps," his fingers were breaking a twig into little pieces but he tried to smile, "one day you will avenge us."

"No," I screamed, "no, I cannot go with the Danes, not with those murderers. I will not eat and sleep and be given orders by the men who killed my father." And in spite of my will, I began to cry; at twelve one is still a child.

"Then, Wulf, I must take you to York. The dogs know us, and I have dropped herbs into the mead so that nobody will wake until morning. You can claim sanctuary at the Cathedral; perhaps they will take you into the Priory school. Only, Egbert will seize your lands. The men have been killed who would have pleaded for you."

"I could die," I sobbed. Nothing would ever be the same again; it would be easier.

13

"No," Leofwen said, "you must make your choice."

"I cannot go to York and sing hymns all day. They would take everything from me, even memory. They would tell me there to pray for my father, not to fight for him."

"If you go as a hostage you will be sent to the main fleet, not to the Danes who were at the ford. Who knows; perhaps in a year or two you will be home."

My collar was choking me; I wiped my eyes with my sleeve. These were vain words, for a hostage seldom returned unless he were ransomed or had the luck to please his lord. By that time most youths had become so Danish that they wanted to remain in their new land.

"I shall ride to the Earls and intercede for you," Leofwen promised.

I shook my head. At least if I left, Leofwen could stay here quietly till he died. "The Earls never keep their word, and you must look after my farm," I said. "I will come back; you must wait for me." Then I buried my head in his cloak so that I should not see the dawn when it came, and wondered how I could suffer such anguish without dying?

ii

THE STABLES smelt of old leather and hay, but at least I was alone. It was the first week that the horses were at pasture, and they had set me to sweep the stalls. "Oh, shall I ever get home?" I muttered as I thrust my broom haphazardly between the irregular cobbles. The dust rose; I sneezed; and my future seemed as blank as this dark corner of the barn.

It would be three years next November since Rollo had fetched me to his castle. At first they had kept me quiet with tales that I should return eventually to Yorkshire. Later, after I had learned the language, I discovered that Rollo had bought me from the Danes to look after his hounds, as coldly as if I had been a serf and not a hostage, because Saxons were famous for their skill with dogs. We were not far from the coast. There was a harbour twenty miles away in Brittany, but the forest between us was a better guard than fifty men-at-arms. It was disputed country; both the Normans and the Bretons claimed it, but nobody lived in the woods except outlaws who killed all solitary intruders lest their paths be betrayed, and the dangerous tree cats whose thick coats blended so well with the dappled branches that a hunter often felt their fangs in his shoulder before he saw them crouched on the boughs above his head. Yet I longed for freedom so much that I knew my chance would come. It narrowed life yet deepened it; for I rejected every thought or experience that I could not link to some possibility of escape.

I stood there, leaning on my broom, desperate with homesickness, while the straw litter lay half swept around me. Suppose, once, when Rollo was hunting, I could dodge into the bushes? The Downs, if I could reach them, were full of viper pits into which it was only too easy to stumble. But there was the river—there must be a path along its banks . . . the words were so near the surface that I jumped guiltily, for a gay voice said, just behind my shoulder, not in Norman-French but in Saxon, "It is much too early in the year to be dreaming about boats."

I looked up in such astonishment that Rafe laughed. He was our new man-at-arms, and had just arrived from his winter turn of guard at the watch-tower by the boundary. "It's simple to read your thoughts," he teased. "If you want to go back to Yorkshire, you have a lot to learn."

"What must I do?" I stammered.

"Wait. Let these March winds and the other alarms settle. I saw two of Lord Odo's men in the wood yesterday; that means trouble." Odo held the land just across the Breton border, and was said to have boasted that he would sack our castle some dark night before we were awake enough to beg for mercy.

"Are you a Saxon?" I asked.

"My mother was. We lost our lands in the fighting up north, and I am thankful that she did not live to see it. The Danes drove down, and the Normans, swearing that they meant to help us, rode up; and after they had looted and burned for a couple of seasons I joined Sir Rollo in order to eat. But I'm a farmer, not a soldier. There may be some relatives of my mother still alive in England. And, anyhow, I'm no happier in a castle than you are."

"Wait how long?" I repeated stupidly. It numbed the mind to hear my own language again after these long, desolate months.

"Till May. But there will be plenty for you to do during the next weeks. Try to be less stubborn and get the others to trust you. Go into the fields as often as you can, and don't waddle across the drawbridge looking back over your shoulder as if you expected an archer to send an arrow through your insides. You might even ask Eudo when you could join the men-at-arms. Then some day, if you are missing for a few hours, nobody will think twice about it. Remember, if your plans should go wrong, there will be no second chance."

"You will really take me with you?"

"That depends on you."

Rafe was taller than Leofwen, and much younger. He could not be more than five years older than myself, but his voice had Leofwen's steadiness and his eyes were the same blue in his windburnt face. "Adapt yourself more to your surroundings so that you are not 'the Saxon' but merely a boy about the castle; keep to your work as much as possible and let them forget you." I must have looked up at him like a drowning puppy (it was the first time for almost three years that anybody had been kind to me), for he added hurriedly, "Never let them see you with me; it might make them suspicious." He patted my shoulder, glanced out of the door to make certain that the yard was empty, and strolled off, swinging a bit of leather as if he had stopped by to fetch a strap. I watched him out of sight, and then went back to my sweeping so light-headed with excitement that for a moment I was willing to be friends even with Rollo himself! What boundary is there to any sky to one who is promised his desire?

It was still cold enough for us to linger through the evenings in the great hall. This was dark and smoky, and except for Sir Rollo and his companions who sat near the fire at the upper end we were never really warm. There was no trace of the easy Saxon atmosphere where ale passed from neighbour to neighbour. The Normans were taciturn; it was almost a point of honour with them not to speak. An old chaplain read an edifying sermon aloud to remind us of our sinfulness, in place of Leofwen's songs. Food and drink were always scarce in this wind-swept land, but even if they had been abundant the soldiers would have made a virtue out of existing upon a crust and a flagon of sour wine. It was one of their constant jokes to say to me, "Oh, that Saxon will eat anything; it is a wonder that he hasn't devoured his own dogs."

I sat at the end of the lowest bench and wished that I were home. Not in the future, not in a dream, but now at this chilly and dismal moment. In spite of the discipline, there was a feeling of uneasiness among us. Something had happened. Eudo had been summoned from his usual seat to wait near Sir Rollo, but until that knight chose to enlighten us it was unsafe to whisper even rumours to each other. We fidgeted with the rushes, and there was a persistent sound of coughing from the victims of the spring cold that had swept from man to man during the last weeks.

"February was dry; we shall have no hay."

"Dry! My old arrow wound told my shoulder it was raining often enough."

"I've known February to be sunnier than March, and yet we've had good pasture."

The voices rose and fell, but no dispute followed. I scratched the straw with the tip of my shoe until I came to the stone pavement. Perhaps it was imagination, but the smoke seemed particularly acrid. It stung my eyes, and I felt that I could hardly breathe.

"Eudo!" We all jumped. It was unnecessary for Rollo to shout when his squire was almost beside him, but we guessed that it was his way of telling us the news. "I have heard that my Lord Odo has his eyes on our lambs. They are fatter than the miserable beasts on those marshes that he pleases to call his land. Better get the herds in to-morrow and double the guard. And remember," his gaze travelled down the benches till I felt that he was staring at the cook boy and myself, "nobody is to leave the castle without my orders."

Perhaps because of the habitual silence, once it was broken everybody talked at once. "Do you think there'll be a siege?" "The ploughing will be late." "Oh, Odo's a raider; he'll carry off a dozen sheep and we shall hear nothing more about him."

"No, he is not a raider." I knew the voice and looked up as Rafe moved to a stool near our bench. "He's been promising the Bretons to restore their old kingdom."

"How do you know?" a man-at-arms asked suspiciously. He was a short fellow with freckles over his hands and face.

"This winter when I was on outpost duty, the wood-cutters spoke to us about it. They say that Odo has offered protection—and plunder—to all the outlaws who will join him. If you count his neighbours as well, he must have nearly a hundred men."

"A hundred men!" One of the soldiers whistled.

"But we have strong walls, a good commander and two wells," Rafe said easily. "It's a very different story to my first siege."

"Where was that?" the man with the freckles grunted.

"Further north. There were only twenty of us in a little tower that you could hardly call a keep."

"Not Sir Rainault's place?" Rafe nodded. "Why, that was more like a heap of stones."

"They almost breached the wall, and we lost a couple of men every day. First the food gave out and then the water. Finally we grew so weak that we slept, even on guard. And then, one night, we never knew why, the enemy rode away. It took all the survivors together to open our gate, and I remember I crawled to a stream and lay there, for half a day, before I could move."

"You were lucky. Those were Northmen."

"Yes, we knew we could expect no quarter. That is why we fought so hard. It was the endless dodging of arrows, the endless climbing up the narrow steps from wall to wall. At the finish I could not even lift my sword. We felt, I suppose, that death was so near to us that nothing more could happen."

Rollo called for wine. Sometimes I had to serve him, but tonight I was lucky; the son of a neighbouring squire was at his table. I leaned back against the wall and watched Rafe through the smoky air that was now almost a fog. He must have spent most of the winter out of doors, because, except for a rim where his hood had covered it, his face was as brown as ours were at midsummer. "We have something to thank Odo for," he joked as the big wine jar passed from hand to hand.

"Oh, you're the fellow that wanders into the forest," our cook said. He was sitting next to me. "It's asking to have your throat cut."

"I only made friends with some woodcutters because their hut was warmer than our tower. Last January, even sitting by the fire I used to wonder if my ears were frozen."

"It's the first time that we have left men there over winter. They moved back before to the castle in October. I suppose my lord knew that there was trouble along the marshes."

"The woodcutters have a strange drink that they make themselves. It induces dreams and heats the blood."

All the soldiers laughed except the man opposite us. He scratched his ear and muttered sulkily, "I wouldn't go into those trees for any drink in the world; they're haunted."

"But there used to be a track to St. Winoc," the cook said, managing to refill his cup before the wine was passed back again. "We rode that way to their fair. It's only recently that it has got so dangerous."

"There's not a trace of a road now," Rafe said decisively. "There is nothing but undergrowth. What do you think of Odo's bowmen?" He turned to the man beside him. "I have always heard that Bretons are good archers."

I looked up and caught Rafe's eye, but he turned his head away almost obviously. Then I knew. He had spent the winter looking for a path. St. Winoc was a little Breton port, not a day's ride in a straight line but impossible to reach without passing through the forest. It was inhabited by sailors and fishermen, and, as far as liberty existed on this bleak coast, they were free. We needed the goods so badly that they carried in their vessels that both Normans and Bretons let them alone. There would be sanctuary and assuredly a boat for England if we could once reach the harbour.

"Wood!" Eudo roared; and several of us sprang up to fetch more logs from the pile beside the door. Many things were turning over in my head at once; new hope, but, to balance it, new danger. "They could pen us here all summer," a man muttered as I passed; "there won't be enough water." We pushed the sticks, one after the other, on to the great fire, and as the sparks flamed and the ashes of the old wood smouldered, I suppose that we were all seeing the same pictures in the blaze. They hooked the long scaling ladder to the wall; a watcher sprawled forward with a dagger through his shoulders; figures crept along the battlements. "You don't know what fighting is," Eudo had often shouted at us, "until a man springs at your throat in the doorway of your room." Then, beyond the clanging and the shouting, as the flames subsided and we turned back to our benches, I saw, but in my own head, waves splashing on the shingle in a little bay. I have to get away, I thought. I have to escape now without waiting any longer. It would be better to die in the woods than be mewed up in these walls, safe perhaps, but lonely, crying as the old cry for a little fluttering warmth. "Tomorrow," the voices mumbled about me, "after the full moon"; and, in a whisper, "it may be a false alarm." They were afraid, in spite of their boasting. I was a stranger, and I seemed to hear, ringing in my ears, the familiar, panted cry, "To arms, Master Rodwen, to arms! The Danes have landed!"

"Can I cross? I want to get some dandelions." The fresh leaves, chopped up in their soup, kept the spring sickness from the dogs.

Eudo's fingers were almost as thick as the bolt that he was greasing, and had the same rusty colour. His steel cap lay on a flat stone near the drawbridge. "It's safer inside than out," he grumbled. "You may bless these walls for sheltering you, in a matter of hours."

The peasants had been streaming towards the castle for the past two days. They had made a little camp in the shelter of the keep, but their herds were left at pasture in the neighbouring meadows. "I could run back a dozen times," I pleaded, "while they are bringing in the flocks."

"Dogs need meat, not grass." Eudo dipped his rag into the grease again and began on a second bolt.

"Last summer I saved a whole litter." Rollo was never tired of repeating that a good dog was worth two serfs, yet he and the other Normans commonly lost their animals for want of a simple knowledge that we Saxons absorbed as children. The great beasts behind me were lying on some sand that had been spilt, the black muzzle of one sleepily buried in its softness, while the other stretched its paw out in a fantastic, heraldic loop. "They are just like a coat of arms," I continued; "have you ever seen Brindle in better coat?" Her heavy squareness on the warm, shimmering gravel imitated the tawny, gold and sable of a banner.

Eudo did not answer. This was usually a signal to us boys to vanish before we were sent upon an errand. Yet I had to get to the fresh grass, away from the stench and barking of the kennels. I shifted the basket on my arm and waited. Finally Eudo looked up. "Run quickly then. If you're not back within the hour, I'll teach you to loiter." We all knew the feel of his heavy fist or staff.

The water plants were only just beginning to grow again in the moat; it was as grey and mournful as a winter morning. Two sentinels in the tower were watching every movement that I made, not because they had guessed what was in my mind but because they had nothing else to do. I cut some plants, held them up, shook them free from dirt and put them deliberately into my basket. Once the watch knew why I was in the fields, I could ramble over to our little stream without suspicion. It was reckless; it was crazy; but from the moment that I had heard Rollo speak of sieges, I had determined to run away.

I might have been able to endure life if I could have spoken to Rafe again, but if I passed him in the courtyard he went on joking with the other soldiers as if I were less to him than the cook boy. Sometimes I wondered if the meeting in the stables had been a dream. The more I had tried to adapt to my surroundings, even though it was to help me in getting away, the more violently I had revolted against everything Norman. I exaggerated the grime and the brutality, and knew that I exaggerated; it was useless, I could not even pretend to accept my fate. "Oh, you monster," I muttered, looking back at the castle, brooding behind its moat. We had laughed at Leofwen's dragon stories; they were only an old man's nightmare of a distant past. Now if he were still alive I could tell him that I had seen one, its claw dug into the earth, visible to a dozen hamlets and able to lash out blindly through its men-at-arms. A boy could be dropped into its dungeons because of a little stolen hare and never see the sun again if its ruler, Rollo, so willed. Why, the Danish raiders seemed a lesser evil here; they plundered, true, but then they sailed away. Yes, it was better to die in the woods, in the clear air and with earth in my hands, than to endure thirst and danger behind those ugly walls.

My hands trembled as I stood up, stretched myself and shook another root. The moment had come. The watch was about to be relieved. They had cleared the ground for half a mile beyond the moat; but the stream was now only a couple of hundred yards in front of me and, if I could reach the shelter of its bank without being seen, I could creep along it until I came to the trees. It would probably be an hour before I was missed; and with Odo at large they would not risk sending out a search party to find a single boy. I started to move, but my feet seemed to catch in the grass. Suppose Odo found me? Would it be a knife thrust, or would they torture me, hung over a fire, because I could not tell them ways into the castle that I did not know myself? Would I lie, like that sheep I had seen once in the undergrowth, while the viper poison struck from the leg to the heart? It was a swift death but more painful, they said, than drowning. Would either be worse than gasping on the castle steps with an arrow through my neck and men trampling over me? It was time. I was wasting daylight. The men had turned away from the parapet to greet their comrades. Run, my brain whispered, run!

Then the bell boomed and there were shouts. Our outposts came riding up. This apparently deserted landscape was full of horsemen and dust. "Help me with the lambs," a shepherd yelled as his dog began to drive the startled, bleating sheep towards the inside of the castle. He could only have been a few lengths away from me. I looked up at the green, thick buds on a hazel that was growing beside the water, but it was too late. The surge of people carried me across the drawbridge, and it was only as I passed Eudo and he shouted, "Make the most of those dandelions; they may be the last you see this season," that I noticed that I was clutching the basket of curling, cress-like leaves against me as if it were a shield.

The landscape ought to have changed. Instead, apart from its emptiness because there was not a calf or an ox-herd visible, it looked exactly the same as it had for months. The gates were closed; the men were at their posts; everybody who could be spared from stabling the beasts was ranged along the walls. I think we were all wondering, now that the ominous clanging of the bell had stopped, if it were a false alarm? Perhaps tomorrow would find us in the fields again, working as if nothing had happened. Then a sentinel shouted, and far off, so far that we saw it only on account of the extreme clarity of the air, a wisp of smoke floated upwards. A barn had been fired.

There were curses. A wail came up from the yard, that hushed into a whimper when Eudo shouted, "Silence!" We watched. Nothing happened for a very long time. I felt a strange breathlessness that did not come from running up the steps, because I had been standing in my place for an hour. Eventually a dark oblong, almost the shape of a cloud, appeared on the horizon.

"There must be a hundred of them; his neighbours have joined him." I started when I heard Rafe's voice. Why had he joined me now after avoiding me for weeks? "Keep away from the walls once the fighting starts," he advised; "you have no armour."

"We have lost our chance of getting away," I moaned, forgetting all caution. "We ought to have left yesterday."

"Yesterday! Are you crazy? Where could we have hidden ourselves? The boats never sail before May. Besides, that forest has been full of Odo's Bretons for weeks, and I would sooner be behind this parapet than in their hands."

Tiny shadows detached themselves from the oblong and separated into individual riders. "Ten, eleven," a man counted from the top of the turret just beyond us. "He has called out the knights all along the coast."

"Sir Rollo is an experienced soldier," Rafe continued gravely, "and I think we ought to beat them off. We have a good stock of food and two wells." Raids were usually timed for the hungriest moment of the year, when the winter stores had been eaten and the new crop was barely sown.

"Rollo!" I shrugged my shoulders. Whenever he passed me by I seemed to hear his noisy bellow, "Never keep the weaklings in a litter, I told you to drown them," or see his evil face as he smashed a puppy's head against the stones.

"Whatever you feel, it is safer to be under his orders at this moment. I like the Bretons, but hungry men make bad enemies; and for twenty years they have been driven out of their lands into the marshes."

The mass was no longer a cloud but a body of men, both mounted and on foot. Their surcoats were black, and they had covered the rest of their armour with a dark substance so that it did not catch the sun. Half a mile away the horsemen drew up in line and galloped slowly towards us. It was the first time that I had ever seen the famous Norman cavalry in action.

"It's a lovely sight," Rafe murmured, "but so wasteful."

"We do not ride to battle," I answered stiffly. "It's unfair."

"The day of single combat is over, Wulf." I looked up in surprise because this was the first time that he had called me by my name. "Unless your Saxons move with the times, I'm afraid that when King Edward dies, freedom will vanish with him."

Rollo was always saying the same thing over his wine. He was certain that Duke William would claim the island. "We shall see your banner on a turret yet," he would shout, slapping his companion on the shoulder. Eudo, for all his twenty years of service, was still a squire; he had no land. "The English won't fight," Rollo would add contemptuously, "they will bargain. Oh, there may be a rising here and there when we begin to squeeze them out, but what can they do once we have built some castles? They will have to serve us or starve. I'm not saying a word against them as farmers, mind you; they have only forgotten how to use a sword."

I had heard the same story as a child in Yorkshire. "Only there is one family," Rodwen had said, "even the Normans cannot conquer." "Not the Earls?" I remember our neighbours had seemed surprised because Edwin and Morkere always moved inland during the summer. It was even whispered that they were not averse to the Danes breaking the power of the coastal franklins; we were too independent for them. Rodwen had shaken his head. "Not the men you mean, but an Earl all the same. Godwin's son, Harald of Kent."

Then we had been silent. Kent and Normandy had both seemed far away. It was almost easier to imagine the Holy Land, when pilgrims, on their way back and forth to York, came to us every sailing season. I should have forgotten the name if my father had not turned to me and said, with one of his rare smiles, "You should remember Earl Harald, Wulf; he is the best falconer in England." At that time (oh, how long ago it seemed), all that had mattered to me was a kestrel that I was trying to tame. I had lost the bird, impetuously flying it too soon, later that summer.

"The Danes still use the axe," I argued.

"Yes, but the power of the Danes is lessening as well. Once the Normans discovered that ten men behind a solid wall could hold up an army, the old values had to change. Where should we be, otherwise, this morning? Aren't you glad," Rafe added laughing, "that we have this parapet here in front of us?"

I pressed my hands upon the stone slabs; they were warm in the sun. Everything seemed static except pain. A tuft of moss grew out of a crack with tiny specklike flowers no taller than a thorn. I had a sudden impulse to uproot it, to burn it decently in the courtyard fire before a body could fall on it or it was shattered by a flying stone. Then I looked over the edge and drew back giddily; the moat was far below us, but they would bring their scaling ladders up to it, smash an entrance perhaps over these very battlements? We Saxons fought man against man in an individual and a courtly struggle according to strict laws. I loathed these Norman men-at-arms, whether they belonged to Rollo or his rival. Their home was a bench in the hall of any commander who had happened to hire them, and it was always the leader, never the land, that mattered.

The invaders drew up just out of bowshot. A dapple of metal rings moved under the dark linen coats. I could not deny their magnificence, in spite of myself. Horses, riders, lances, all moved as one, and the great, multi-coloured banner fell into serpent folds, now that there was no wind, above its bearer.

"What will happen now?" I asked.

"As they have not surprised us, they will send a herald. Claim the land, I suppose, because somebody's great-grandfather did homage for it. We shall have to fight and endure," Rafe continued cheerfully. "There is nothing else to do." Then he added, as if to soften the blow, "Once Odo is out of the way, it will be a much safer ride to the coast."

A figure, probably the herald, detached itself from the mass. I was too impatient to listen to his meaningless words; it was not my war. There would be no mercy if Odo stormed the castle. I should be killed as swiftly as any of the others, but I hated anything and everything Norman so much that even at such a moment of extreme danger I felt no loyalty towards Rollo. Wherever I looked, I saw peasants clinging to the walls and chattering as if this panoply of force were a procession for them to watch and applaud. Below me a woman screamed about a lost hen; children were playing games in the space around the keep. How different it was from our Saxon fashion, man matched against man, under the open sky! "Our way is better," I muttered to Rafe. "Taking arms from these herdsmen has turned them into fools." Well, they could watch their parade until the first arrow hurtled through the air. I would stand here no longer. We could not even hear the messenger's words. I wanted what was to come to us to happen, if only I could step now to the other side of the event and have it over; whatever its outcome, it would be easier than this uncertain pause. "I must go down to the kennels," I said, and at that moment the trumpet sounded again. It meant that the parley had ended.

It was suddenly still. It had not been so quiet for days. There had always been shouts, a horse neighing, the hollow sound when men rushed down from the keep and their armour banged against the wall. Even the chickens forgot to clack, and the children to whimper; as I leaned forward to look out of the partly opened door, the rustle of the straw below me made me jump.

This was the fifth week of the siege, and the wells were beginning to dry up, so that we suffered terribly from thirst. The morning when we had watched Odo's men gallop over the meadow seemed unbelievably far away. Where Rafe was, I did not know; and I was not able to look for him. Steps and passages had to be kept clear so that men could move easily from one part of the defences to the other; and I got an instant clout from the first soldier I met if I ventured into the courtyard except at dawn and dusk when I fetched a meagre allowance of food and water to the kennels. At first I had had plenty to do to keep the hounds quiet. Lack of movement and the exciting scents and noises had driven them frantic until they had all but tugged their chains from the iron rings. Now, subdued by lack of food, they lay in utter submission on the dirty rushes that smelt worse every day, hardly pricking up their ears if an archer passed or a stone dropped in the yard.

Leofwen had said, "Axes break no runes." Like all his proverbs this was partly true because his sayings had been all the consolation that I had had in Normandy. But now, at this moment, words had lost their power. "Batter it

31

enough and the strongest link will break," the armourer's old joke, was nearer to my mood. If I had exerted myself I might have found a few half-clean rushes to make a softer bed; but though my mind was active, my body seemed paralyzed. I could only plait a thong and unplait it again in a numb, continuous misery, knowing all the time that it was easier for me than for the frightened serfs huddled among their cattle in the courtyard. Odo or Rollo—what did a name mean to them? They were in the castle's power, bound, poor wretches, if the world turned upside down, to a squire's orders and the same strip of land. I, the hostage, the Saxon, had something not a man among them could imagine, the memory of boyhood in a free civilization. Naturally I pitied them, but personal emotions are always stronger than reason; sitting in the half-kennel, half-dungeon, in a light so dim that nobody had seen the real colour of the walls, I longed for an arrow to end my despair even more than I wanted Odo's soldiers to be defeated.

I had listened so long for footsteps that when they came I never heard Rafe until he stood beside me. "If you stay here much longer," he teased, flicking my thong playfully, "you'll turn into a dog yourself."

I glanced up at his steel cap and saw, to my relief, that it was still undented. "Why is it so quiet? What has happened?"

"Nobody knows. Henry stood up carelessly, and an arrow grazed his shoulder; there are fires burning, and guards before their camp, but Eudo swears he saw horsemen moving towards the woods. If so, they may have left a rearguard to persuade us that we are still besieged, while their main force retires."

"Why don't we make a sortie?"

"Too dangerous." Rafe shook his head. "It could be a trick to persuade us to open the gate. Odo may have ridden off to welcome reinforcements. No, as soon as it is dark, Roger will swim across the moat, circle round and signal us. If they have withdrawn we are lucky; there isn't a week's food left."

"And what have we gained?" I asked bitterly.

"Nothing. We've lost four men and several serfs; all the fields will have to be re-sown; it will be a hungry winter. Still, we have our lives." Rafe was irritatingly cheerful. "It might have been worse."

"Not for me. I cannot endure this any longer."

"If Odo has really gone," Rafe bent down anxiously as if he were afraid that even the cracked stones under the straw were listening to us, "we are going to attack his rearguard. To loot some horses, I suppose, and relieve our feelings. Go to the stables as soon as it gets dark. Say you needed a strap for the dogs or that you were told to help saddle if anybody questions you. Be careful, though I doubt if they will count the riders; they have already started drinking to our victory. Be sure not to join me too soon—it might look suspicious—but follow me when I turn. Last winter I found a track; you'll see it on the right as we enter the woods; it leads down to the coast."

I jumped up so suddenly that a dog growled, and Rafe shook his head. "Quiet, you will ruin our chances if you are so impetuous. You are not to move before nightfall; and, then, push this well down over your head." He thrust a steel cap into my hands, looked out again to make sure that nobody was watching us, and hurried off to his post.

33

It was May. All the air was field flowers that had grown uncut. The noise, the terror and the dirt of the past days were over; we thundered across our drawbridge into paradise. The horses kicked and plunged after being inactive for so long, and I saw Eudo bring a heavy, mailed hand cruelly down on his charger. We fanned out so as to have extra space; there were no obstacles before us. I was in love with the scents—this was timothy grass, that cloverwort or was it sorrel? Even the hooves fell lightly on the turf. We were free. We were riding faster than I had ever galloped. You cannot imagine happiness, I thought, or even remember it afterwards. It is passion; it flames in the blood as scaldingly as those wine drops from Rollo's cup that burnt my hands last December when he spilled them over me. Free . . . free . . . free . . . the moment only; there is no is-to-be, no what-has-been. All that troubled me was the too-large steel cap that slipped over my eyes. I snatched it off recklessly; what if the other men noticed? They would think that I wanted to earn a place in their company; who of them would dream that I was on my way home?

We swept towards the left to avoid the tents and any possible trap. There had been little fighting on this side. I had seen a body near the willows in the moat, a serf, for he wore no armour; and we passed a man, rolled over and clasping distorted knees, under an old tree stump. It was good not to be in the main field; it must have been littered with bodies from the day when they had tried to bring up the scaling ladders and had been driven back. As it was, our speed started a little wind, and there was a smell of death and damp, charred wood in our nostrils as we drew level with their camp, though we were yards from the spot where they had pitched their tents.

We thundered forward. Get away, get away, the hooves beat on the grass. What did it matter if I had to die; we should have had this ride. Was this the spell, the madness, that made men forget their heritage and brought them shouting to the Norman banner? Hunters only skirmished with danger; ploughmen never knew this ecstasy. It was the nearness, almost the certainty of dying, of being swung on a lance tip into a branch like the fellow whose body we had just passed, that united the senses into some triumph beyond the apprehension of ordinary men. Yes, I almost shouted aloud, we have torn the surcoat from the armour; this is what life is, not resignation but . . . Being! There were three shameful years to purge. "Don't let Wulf carry the sword; he will drop it," as of course I had, from very hatred. "Keep that greedy Saxon fellow out of the kitchen," when I had only gone there to beg some bones for the dogs. The insults numbered themselves, one after the other, until I felt my dagger hilt, kicked my horse's flanks, passed two other riders and drew abreast of Rafe.

"Careful," Rafe grunted, "not so fast. Rein back a bit; we must be the last into the woods."

I glanced round. Eudo, being better mounted, was a long way in front. The field itself was still level, but the soft, dark edges of the forest rose now like a keep out of the valley. "I heard Eudo say that he was taking the short cut so as to surprise them at the river. We turn to the right—if we can."

It was not so easy. Eudo kept glancing over his shoulder in the moonlight, and there were a dozen men around us. I had put on my steel cap again, and nobody hailed me. The trees came nearer and nearer; the horses slowed down of themselves; presently we entered a forest track, riding one after the other and occasionally ducking to avoid a stray bough. Rafe was in front of me, but a Norman whom we had not noticed came up behind us. I dared not stop; even if I pretended that my saddle girth had slipped, he would draw up to help me. A struggle would bring his comrades back at once. I could see the clearing a few yards ahead where the other path forked towards the sea. Rafe turned round, saw the fellow and looked at me helplessly. I stared as helplessly back. I would rather die, I knew, than stay another day with Rollo. Should I stop? Should I turn? What did Rafe himself want to do? I could not think fast enough, a moment more and we should be past the turning. Then the Norman brushed past us both, so unexpectedly that my pony stumbled and a branch knocked my cap sideways. I was about to curse him, I was so startled, when I saw Rafe swing to the right. Every sound doubled. I felt sick; surely Eudo must have heard those crashing twigs? I held my breath; we rode ten yards, twenty yards, gradually the sound of the other hoof beats lessened in the distance. "Kind of Étienne to do that," Rafe whispered as I drew level with him at a clearing. "It gave us our chance."

"Did he know?" I asked in surprise, and Rafe nodded. "He must have guessed."

It was twenty miles to the port, and we had at most till dawn before Eudo discovered that his Saxons had disappeared. Still, Odo's retreat had driven those outlaws who had not joined him into hiding, and for this one night we could ride openly and safely through the forest. Neither of us spoke again; we trotted along the narrow track as fast as we dared. My exultation had gone. I would look up, see a figure watching us, and start, only to find that it was the shadow of a bush. So much could happen before we reached open ground. My throat was dry; I tried to hold my breath as if I were below a wave and would drown unless I waited for the surface and the light. It was morning, and our tired beasts had dropped into a walk before we came out to the cliffs and saw three ships anchored in the blue cove below them. "Oh, Rafe," I shouted, while the gulls dipped and wheeled over our heads, "look, that must be St. Winoc. We're free!"

iii

B ROTHER THOMAS LIVED FOR HIS FLOWERS.
I swung my sack of pebbles to the ground before I
opened the gate that led into the Priory. We had patched
the paths in the autumn, but the rains had washed away
the smaller stones and nettles sprouted from the runnels.
I untied the leather thong at the mouth of the bag and
tipped my load into the centre of the track. I might have
been a child dropping shells! The mud absorbed lumps
the size of my fist, and I rubbed my shoulder, wondering
if Brother Thomas would realize the weight that I had
carried simply for the privilege of watching him paint?
Actually it was a favourite penance of the Abbot to set
the villagers to work filling up this hole. There was a
"close time" for sin over harvest and dry weather, but
during the wet months they had to pay for every slight
misdeed by bringing up stones to the accompaniment of
prayers. I would willingly have dragged up six sacks for
a single drawing, but I resented the mixing up of wicked-
ness and road mending. Evil was not a thing to be wiped
out with a mumble and a heave; it had to be faced like a
raider and fought. I suppose it was true (as many people
whispered) that I belonged to the "old religion" at heart.
Fortunately in this remote part of Cornwall the priests

did not worry us much, provided that we paid our tithes and came to their main services. I tried to wipe the worst of the dirt from my shoes and then knocked lightly at the wicket gate.

"Come in," a voice answered; "it's unlatched." The dogs knew me and barked a welcome from the kennels. The bare boughs of a week before were now a delicate green. I walked past the barn and through the orchard towards the dove cote and the inner garden. In a few days it would be full spring.

Brother Thomas was sitting on the low stone wall that divided the apple trees from the herbs. He had a wooden board on his lap, but his eyes were fixed on five white stars growing in the sheltered bed that ran the length of the stables. "A day like this," he called, without looking up, "I said to myself, it's Wulf."

"How are the onions?" I asked cheerfully, and he shuddered. It was one of our pretended quarrels. He would use Latin words for our many little worts and even called the fragrant maythe, camomile!

"There are five flowers this year; last spring there were three."

"And five years ago, when you watched us wade ashore, there were none."

"Is it really five years?"

"In May. I remember I was too sea-sick to care what happened; and then we sailed into calmer water and Rafe made me sit up. He told me that we were safe because the captain knew the cove, but I wasn't interested in anything till we landed."

Brother Thomas laughed and made a place for me to sit beside him on the wall. "And now you go out fishing," he said, moving a pot of brushes.

39

"Only when it is calm." The choppy waves and under-currents by the mackerel rocks often sent me to lie ignominiously at the bottom of the boat.

"It's a long time," the monk said, putting down his board. "You came the summer that I painted my first picture. I had just been sent here from the Missal School at Bodmin, and I daubed paint over all the refectory wall. Last year the Abbot let me block it out and begin over again. I had misjudged my space, I remember, and had to turn an angel's head into a dove." His brush made a line in the air as if he were still measuring the surface. "I thought I knew everything, and I had to learn humility through staring three full winters at the result, but . . . ," he added with a sigh, "I have never been so happy."

I nodded. There were too many memories. I could see myself standing on deck, and our captain rowing ashore. Leofric was running down to meet him, in the same old jerkin that he still wore when it rained. Then I was following Rafe up a winding path between banks of fragrant grasses full of bees. I heard Laurel's voice for the first time, "But how was it possible to escape from Normandy?" I felt old Estrith's hands pulling off my wet coat in the kitchen. "Sometimes I feel that I have lived here all my life; and then come moments when it seems like yesterday."

"That is because you are happy." Brother Thomas took his drawing up again. "Only, you must stop breaking your heart about Yorkshire."

I had never been back, and it worried me.

"Suppose you were able to claim your land—and after eight years who is going to recognize you? What is there

40

to gain but loneliness? Here you have work and friends; why, they treat you like a son of the family!"

"I am very, very grateful." Laurel's uncle (she was his ward) had taken Rafe and myself to live at Nansvean. "It is just the satisfaction of getting the ground he stole away from Egbert. I have my hostage rights."

Brother Thomas shook his head. "From what the Abbot tells us there are many disorders in the North. What justice would you get unless you had an army with you?"

"I could sell the farm and come back with a belt full of gold pieces," I continued. "Then I could buy a bit of land here." This was a dream, and I knew it. Every year, as King Edward had grown weaker, the roads had become more dangerous. "If it were just a question of journey money I would give it to you freely," Laurel's uncle had said to me over and over again; "but as things are, unless you hired an escort, you would be murdered long before you got to Winchester."

"Pride," Brother Thomas grunted, "pride; but as I've told you, I suffered from it too. That's your failing, Wulf. God has spared you from many dangers, but you are still discontented. What does it matter who the land belongs to, if the farmer is good? Take your feelings out in crops and not in boundaries."

I watched the outline of another flower appear on the board. It was not really the question of my land, though I could not say this to Brother Thomas. I never wanted to see my father's farm again. The shock that autumn day had been too great. Looking back, it seemed to me that I had always known, a skin beneath the surface of my mind, that it was a temporary dwelling, not my home.

41

Perhaps my father's loneliness, after my mother's death, had seeped into the fields? It was Leofwen who worried me. At my happiest moments I remembered him; I had even run after an old beggar with a dozen eggs because something about him had reminded my of my teacher's shoulders. Leofwen had been so old that I felt sure he must have died long before my Norman captivity had ended. Only, ought I not to go and see, hear at least what had happened to him, to whisper over his grave (as if that made any difference!) that I had obeyed him and returned? It was foolish; it was throwing away the real love of Rafe and Laurel, my settled place by Nansvean fireside, for an imaginary pilgrimage. Yet until I made this journey, should I be ever utterly at peace?

I dared not speak of this to Brother Thomas. I had poured the whole story out to him our first spring, and we had quarrelled so bitterly that we had not spoken again for almost a year. "Leofwen," he had sneered. "It was the mercy of God that you were taken from him to Normandy. Rollo's soldiers were rough men but they feared God. Why, the fellow was a pagan, a harper, filling your innocent mind with dreadful, wicked songs! I wonder what your father was about, to allow him on the place; except that your father, poor man, was so constantly on guard duty that he probably did not realize what was happening to you." I had not trusted myself to speak; I had simply got up and walked away, realizing for the first time the gulf that existed between the Priory and myself. Neither the Latin prayers nor the sign of the hammer meant anything to me. It was the hearts of people that mattered, whether they had pity and understanding. I should never have gone back if Rafe had not sent me over, months later, with our tithe of apples, and Brother

Thomas had not met me and shouted gaily as if nothing had happened, "Can you spare a moment, Wulf, to help me move a bush? These fisher boys tear the roots away from the ground instead of dislodging them." Since then I often came over if I had no other task, because I loved to watch him paint; but we had never spoken again about Yorkshire.

"Well, is Leofric going to find you some more onions this summer?" I asked lightly, for we were dangerously close to the forbidden subject. "Have you discovered yet what they are called?"

"No, they are in neither of our leech books. Leofric says that they do not grow in Brittany; all he knows about them is that he bought them from a pilgrim there. He wanted to bring me a gift because I had cured his cough. He thought they were vegetables."

"You will have to send a bulb to Bodmin," I suggested.

"Oh, no! It would be impossible to disturb them until they are well rooted in this soil."

I smiled. He was afraid that if the Bishop saw one he would demand the bulbs. It had happened once before with a specially scented rose. "The Abbot is not certain that they are Christian flowers," the monk continued gloomily, "and I want to paint them outside St. Christopher's hut in our new missal. Leofric had to explain about the pilgrim before I got permission."

I longed to ask him what the difference was between a Christian and a pagan flower. I suppose he meant a plant found only in heathen lands, but it was unkind to tease him too much. "The new missal! I thought you told me at our last meeting that you would have no time for painting this summer?"

There were never enough hours to paint, dig, dry

herbs and look after the sick villagers. The Abbot was always promising to get a boy to help with the garden; but then the Priory roof would leak, or a cow would die, and there would be no spare gold.

"Sometimes a good deed springs indirectly from an evil one. Haven't you heard about the wine?"

"The wine! No, but it's a week since I was down in the village."

Brother Thomas frowned. He was suspicious when I went rambling alone across the moor. The "Goon" as we called it in Cornish (it meant a glaze of even colour, whether on sea or land) was a symbol to him of disorder, smuggling and the "sacred trees" against which the Abbot waged unending war. Actually we had been busy with the spring ploughing so that my conscience was clear. "We were working up in the Long Field," I explained. "The weather delayed us; it has been so unsettled."

Brother Thomas looked relieved.

"Well, Osric lost a lamb; and searching for it he found three casks of wine at the *top* of the cliff. Miraculous, wasn't it, for the casks to be washed up so far above sea level? The Abbot said that it was God's gift because that particular cave was on our land. He sold them for five gold pieces, and when Osric is better he is coming to work in the garden."

"Why, what happened to Osric?"

"On the night of the discovery he was severely beaten going home."

"To teach him to keep his mouth shut"; and we both laughed. Neither the Bretons nor ourselves saw why we should pay tithes on goods bought with so much hardship and danger. Ships sailed to Brittany every summer from the villages along the coast, and their vessels visited us in return. We sent them fish, honey and sometimes hunting dogs; they shipped us wine and corn. "What a lot each of us owes to Leofric," I said, looking at the flowers again. "You know, he recognized our captain when we landed."

Even Rafe's practical mind had conceded that our journey had had something of the miraculous about it. We had been bound for the port thirty miles to the east when a strong wind had blown us into the cove. Plenty of fishermen on both sides of the water plundered any vessel blown out of its course, and we had unsheathed our weapons. Then a man had waved to us from the beach. Leofric had remembered our rigging from his previous visit to Brittany, so they had welcomed us, not as strangers but as brothers.

"It's hot today," I grumbled, edging towards the shade while Brother Thomas put his board down for the second time and leaned back lazily. The sun seemed to burn the primroses; they looked faded under a sky that was the same intense blue as the cake of paint that the monk kept only for St. Christopher's robe. "A week ago it was so wet that we could hardly plough, and now it might be June."

"It's the comet," Brother Thomas answered gravely. "Whenever the seasons are disordered, Man is disordered too; they follow each other in a mutual fever." I nodded, deep in my own thoughts. Of course I did not believe old Estrith's story that it was a portent to call us to repentance because the men had got drunk at Candlemas and a silly girl had run off with a fisher boy, but I was uneasy all the same. Why had it flashed in awful terror across the sky just after they had chosen Harald? If it could have come before King Edward's death instead of afterwards, it would have predicted doom assuaged instead of doom to come.

"The times are unsettled to match," the monk continued. "I fear we shall look back upon King Edward's reign as most of us look back upon our childhood."

I did not reply. There had been too many Normans at the court. They had weakened and disrupted us for years. A man who assumed their ways and spoke their language was on the road to riches, while the loyal thane who got himself killed fighting raiders on our borders never got enough during his lifetime to replace the axe he had blunted in the king's service. "It is a terrible thing for a man to break his oath," Brother Thomas went on, altering a line with his brush; "but the Abbot says that he knows the Duke is merciful, and that if the Earl would confess his fault he would leave him second in the kingdom."

"He would never do that," I said scornfully. Nobody was more arrogant than the Duke, and he feared Harald's military leadership. Only the Norman was crafty; he could conceal his feelings, and he had always courted the Church. "Besides, an oath can only be binding if a man is free to take it. King Harald was a prisoner and trapped."

"An oath sworn above relics, and such holy ones, is always sacred to God."

Was it possible that any God would want a man to betray himself or his people through a trick? I waited until the monk had finished another leaf with precise and tiny strokes, because it was dangerous to say aloud what I really felt. Then I stooped to pick up a brush that had rolled under a shrub and murmured, "King Edward had sent Harald to Normandy as his messenger; he was entitled to protection."

"That is one story. Others say that he went off wilfully on a hunting party; and anyhow it was not the Duke who captured him."

"The Lord of Evreux was the Duke's man, and after Harald reached the Duke's court he was not allowed to leave it."

"We do not know what really happened," Brother Thomas wiped a thread of ochre from his brush, "but it was King Edward's will that the Duke should succeed him."

"It was not for him to choose," I reminded the monk. "It is our right as Saxons to say who shall lead us."

"And if you choose invasion and ruin?"

"We shall die free; men across the Channel are serfs."

How I wished that Brother Thomas would not destroy the peace of the day! Some doves were flying about the yard, but it was too early for the bees. I should have liked to sit here drowsily while the shadows moved to late afternoon, but if I stayed we should only quarrel again. I yawned, stretched myself and grumbled, "I suppose I ought to go back and help bring in the cows, but this weather makes me sleepy."

He went on painting for a few moments without a word. "Look at that white; try as I will, I cannot get the colour. It is transparent and solid at the same time, of course; it is partly the sun behind the petal." Then he sighed and stood up himself, rubbing his hands with a bit of rag. "Come to the dispensary first, and I'll give you a handful of feverfew, boiled with wine; it is excellent for all spring fevers. I am taking it myself every evening."

"I suppose the Abbot had no news?" We were sitting round the fire after supper and Rafe leaned forward to put on more wood.

"No, what can we expect before the fairs begin?" In this "island within an island," as the Abbot called our part of Cornwall, the great moors shut us off from England. It was often autumn before we knew what the Witan had decided during the spring. To compensate, sailors brought us gossip from the tip of the windy Flanders coast to the rim of the Breton marshes. We had heard, for instance, that Rollo had brought the attack on his castle before the Duke, and that William had rewarded him for his tenacity by giving him a post in the army. "It is a pity," Rafe said uneasily, "that King Edward could not have lived for another year."

"Osric heard something in the village today," Estrith remarked.

"Oh, Osric!" We all laughed, and Estrith, who liked him because he gossiped with her, looked indignant.

"What did he say?" Laurel asked soothingly. She had the most beautiful voice that I had ever heard. The way she said some ordinary phrase could haunt my ears as continuously as the stream flowing over the ferns at Rosmellyn in summer.

"They were kneeling round the King's bed at Westminster, thinking that his sufferings were over, when he sat up suddenly and shouted in terror that he had seen what would happen to England."

"And did he tell them his vision?"

"Yes; the Red Dragon was lying on the ground in the battle dust."

"Old wives' tales." Rafe was prompt and scornful. "Any man so ill would have fevers and delusions."

"You may laugh," Estrith was angry, "but wait; it will be as he said; dying men see true; now I remember . . ."

"It might have been a Norman messenger," I suggested hastily, because if Estrith started rambling it would go on until bedtime. "They must have wanted to spread panic among the villages so that we should not elect Earl Harald King."

"If there should be a compromise," Rafe continued calmly, "and the Duke became our nominal ruler, would it affect us here in Cornwall so much? They need fish, but only the Bretons are sailors. There would be heavier tithes and they would enroll some of our young men in their bands, but they would let us alone if there were no resistance, at least at first."

"We shall resist," I said.

"Why must men make wars?" Laurel looked up appealingly, but her old uncle was drowsing in his chair. "I want no changes at Nansvean."

"There would be this consolation," Rafe went on. "Penda would have to mend his lawlessness if the Duke came to power."

"Penda!" Estrith shrieked. "Don't mention that name." She even jumped up and tried the bolted door as if she fancied that his men were already in the yard. The dogs stirred uneasily, and the old man opened his eyes and said, "What's that?"

"Nothing." Laurel bent over and tucked the woollen coverlet about his knees again. "We were just talking about Westminster."

The man had terrified our corner of the world. He was a short, dark, changeable fellow; some people said that his mother had been an Irish captive brought back from a raid, and others that a blow on the head in a fight had driven him crazy. Nobody could charge him with being a heretic, because, when the women mumbled, he pointed to his large and frequent gifts to the Church. Nor could we speak openly of him as a bandit. How were we to prove that it was his men who had killed two pedlars on a supposedly safe road, or that he was responsible for robbing a farm while the men were ploughing and the women in the dairy? All we knew for certain was that gradually trader after trader sought him out to pay for their protection as they moved from fair to fair. Then the prices of even a wooden comb or strip of leather doubled. He would ride into a market place, buy a basket of cakes and toss them to the children; the next day he would turn an old woman out of her house on some more or less legal pretext and leave her to beg on the roads. I, myself, had seen him give a younger man a horse, lend another a falcon. He drained his lands for his great feasts; but, after they were over, there was always another young fool who had gambled away his inheritance and had the choice between joining Penda's band or going into exile. He terrorized the countryside, but our villages would not unite; and west of Bodmin there were not forces enough to check him.

A pedlar in some ale-house brawl had heard an ominous story. While two men were quarrelling about their flocks, one of Penda's band had shouted that they had better fatten their beasts instead of fighting over them; because his master intended to marry that girl over at Nansvean and they would need the lambs for the marriage feast. As long as Laurel's uncle was alive, he had so many friends at Bodmin that we felt protected; but he was old and ailing now, and at his death Laurel would inherit the richest lands in the valley. The village hoped that she would marry Rafe. Although he was a stranger, there was something in his manner that made everybody love him. "He knows how to defend us," I had heard people say. "And look how skilful he is with the land."

People were too ready to talk, I felt, as the flames crackled and somebody put another log on the fire. Laurel, like myself, needed freedom. Instead of joining the other girls in their games, she preferred to roam about the cliffs, looking for tiny leaves to pound and boil into dyes. It was only after she had made Brother Thomas a yellow that he swore was the best that he had ever used, and the Abbot had sent some of her colours to Bodmin, that she had been allowed to develop this gift. Her uncle and Rafe admired her skill without understanding it; and Estrith, who had brought her up after her mother's death, frankly hated what she called "those messy jars and silly patterns." Her rippling wools and linens were too imaginative. She copied the fragile red of a weed floating on a narrow wave or the faint green of an acorn point, while the women here wanted the same bright blues and scarlets that they had been wearing for a century.

Oh, Estrith, I wanted to explain, look at life's weaving; it has so few simple colours in it. What is this choice of a king at the far end of England but part of our nearer, particular problem of Penda's lawlessness? Suppose, while the reeves are at Bodmin swearing their oath to Harald, we wake to find these walls on fire and Penda's bowmen up there in the woods, waiting to pick us off, one by one, as we stumble into the yard? Or, if this does not happen and we are summoned to arms, you and Mistress Laurel will be under the Abbot's protection with the rest of the village women. Yet he himself is trying to uproot our independence and replace it with the Norman obedience.

Yes, one swathe follows the other and is knotted to it; nothing is simple, not even for you or the babies by the hearth.

We sat in the warm room and nobody spoke for a time, but I heard the wind crackling in the elms beyond the barn. "They waited in the Great Hall for their doom." Now it was Leofwen's voice that rang in my memory. "Every man stood with his thoughts; there was neither anger nor confusion, but if you could have asked a stranger about their silence, what could he have spoken of but snow?" Shadows, all of us shadows, Leofwen's face (and who would remember him once I was dead), the present firelight, everything was shadowy but pain.

I shivered; this was no good omen. Leofwen had sung the tale, and we had thought not about men but about the last battle between the more than mortals, the day before the landing of the Danes.

"Well, we shall hear in good time," Rafe said, stretching his long legs towards the hearth. Then he added with that touch of vision that often startled me and that made our daily grumbles seem insignificant, "I am more afraid of Earl Tostig than of the Duke; we are a marrow bone between two snarling dogs."

Laurel gripped her chair; Estrith gasped. We had all forgotten about the North. Of course I knew that Earl Tostig had gone into exile after quarrelling with his brothers; he was a proud man, people said. The other Godwins thought of England or of their family, but he was like someone from another age, ruthless, with a mind set on war. It seemed so far from our small village. Wasn't it enough to have to wonder whether the old pear tree would crack in the next gale or if the cattle plague would creep to our fields from Bodmin?

"We are so unprepared," Rafe continued. Then he added—to my surprise, because, like myself, he seldom spoke now of the days before Cornwall—"It is the Yorkshire Earls that have brought this evil on us. What were they doing, Wulf, to let your father and hundreds like him be slaughtered piecemeal? Where was their fleet? Hunted away, I suppose, while they bribed their lawless folk with feasts instead of training them to be soldiers."

I was silent, thinking of this new danger. Must everything be destroyed once more just as we had the illusion that we were happy? Then Laurel's uncle nodded, and Rafe took the best silver cup from its place on the wall. "We had better chase these gloomy thoughts away with a little wine. The sky looks unsettled again, and I want to start sowing as soon as it is light tomorrow. If we have to go to Bodmin later on, to swear allegiance to King Harald," (I knew that he spoke of this rather than mention war in front of Laurel), "the more tasks we have behind us the better. It's going to be wet this season, if I know anything about the weather."

The spring reflected Rafe's words. We had dreary weeks of drizzling rain, separate, unbearably hot days; then, just as we had expected the weather to settle down, a black frost cut the blossoms from the trees. We blamed the comet. Even the Abbot admitted that it might cause storms, though he preached on Sunday against those country fools who whispered old prophecies to each other while they cut the hay. Pedlars came to the fairs with stories of ships gathering in the north; there was talk of men being needed at Bodmin for the Channel Watch. Yet we could not live indefinitely in this atmosphere of danger, and by midsummer the village had forgotten our national peril in their personal disasters. Crops failed; cattle died; within living memory no farmer had known so disastrous a year.

It was July before the sun was strong enough to dry out our meadows and then we had a second, false spring that made us all restless. My favourite tasks of the previous year turned into burdens. I wanted to be afoot among the moors, wandering where I willed, and not bound to a yoke of oxen and the same, never changing fields.

"Go and see if there is any news of the boat coming back from Brittany," Rafe said to me one sultry afternoon. "Leofric is sure to have something to tell us."

I sprang up, only too thankful to be free for an hour, and was halfway down the lane before Rafe shouted, "Are you in love? That's the second time you've left the gate open. I don't want the cows trampling the little barley we have left."

"In love!" My voice was as indignant as my feelings. "No; but it's true that I was thinking about something else. I'd like to go with the fleet myself before I settle to be only a farmer."

"You are never only a farmer; either the land is in you or it isn't. With you, Wulf, I have often felt that a time would come when you wanted to leave this," and he looked as lovingly at the wild sorrel creeping up the bank as I would have looked at a painted arras. "But this year we have to be patient."

"The Duke will come," I said. "I have always known it. With Rollo, with his followers."

Rafe stooped down to pull out a weed that had grown between the posts of the gate. "No," he answered, "I am not so sure. He can fight Harald or he can fight Norway, but even his horsemen cannot manage two armies. I think he will let Tostig and the King cut the death runes on each other; then he will step in and take the prize. Once Harald were dead, the Duke could have England without a battle."

I shook my head. "We should never accept him," I repeated.

Rafe shrugged his shoulders; he was prodding the earth with a short stick. "Look, Wulf, a few inches down, the soil is as water-logged as ever. It will take weeks before the fields are properly dry. I would rather plough a meadow than follow any king to battle, but we may have years more of this uneasy truce; so stop wondering about the world and go and have a swim. This is the best day that we have had all summer."

It was because the air was so still and dry that I waited a moment. The thought of a Norman ever setting foot in our valley spoilt my holiday. I looked at the turf, all thyme and honey with a crust of salt over it from the gales, and I must have shaken my head because Rafe shouted teasingly as I turned, "Really, you must be in love."

The leaves had grown together above the path; and sunlight, falling through the crevices, turned the dusty road into patterns that Brother Thomas might have painted on his wall. Here was the hub of a wheel, there a horseshoe; once, where a bough had broken away, leaving two twigs upright, I could imagine shadowy pigeons perched on the top of a hedge. A dozen impulses struggled in my mind at once; I loved Nansvean but I wanted to ship with Leofric; I was afraid of Normandy and our own future. Then as if these questionings were not enough, under them all, just as continuously as the stream thudded, a few yards away, among the stones, I thought of York-shire. Ought I to return? Ought I to stay here? Duty was not a simple matter of following a leader. I was ready to fight either Norman or Dane, but I could not face those intangible things: neither the ford where they had found my father, nor the courtyard where they had lain him.

"Master Wulf!" Egwin was standing where the track forked sideways. One part went to the village, and the other along to the mill. He had on his new jerkin; and remembering Rafe's words to me, I wondered if he were courting some girl. "Master Wulf, are you going to Tre-woon? When we fetched the pigs the other day, I must have left my knife there."

Trewoon was a distant farm that stood on the edge of the moors. I was often sent across to help Thorkell, the reeve, at the harvest or the ploughing season, and some-times I slipped over in the autumn to join him for a day's fowling. He was the best hunter in the district. "No," I answered, "not today. It's too hot, I'm going swimming."

"It must be hot if you complain." My hatred of the cold was a village joke. "But remember, it's unhealthy to get salt on the skin before the sun goes down." Egwin's dislike of water was equally proverbial. "Better come and sit in the shade with me. This weather isn't fit for man or beast, but our sins have brought it on us." He bleated the last words like a pious old woman muttering phrases from a sermon while she scrubbed her washing.

I shook my head and laughed. Egwin was bound for the ale house, and to get rid of him I pressed a small coin into his hand. "You can do my drinking for me," I said. "I'm going to find a shady rock and sleep until it is cool enough to bathe."

"Mistress Laurel went towards Rosmellyn with her

basket," he muttered, as if he wanted to thank me for giving him the token. "She's lonely today, with Master Rafe working up in the field."

I did not reply and he went off happily, bellowing something about the dangers of swimming by moonlight. I sat down on a warm boulder half-covered with thyme, and waited until his squat figure was out of sight. It was absurd to let myself be irritated by a few foolish words. Egwin's gossip was never kind, but he had made me angry. How dared he suggest that Rafe and Laurel were ordinary people, in love with one another. For five years they had been my inseparable companions. We guessed each other's thoughts; we had never had a quarrel. I worshipped Laurel as we all worshipped her. This was something as natural as the stars shooting across the vault of darkness. One day, after her old uncle was dead, people would come as if on pilgrimage from Bodmin to see her splendid linens. Rafe would farm, and I should be in the background, a balance between them both, to love and serve them; unless, meanwhile, my conscience drove me to Yorkshire. We were comrades, if I had to put so tenuous and perfect a relationship into words.

I was too restless to sit long, and after a few moments I started across to the mill. There was something about the waves seen from this level that was utterly unlike the sweep of ocean visible from the cliffs. If I stared long enough at these rollers that lingered before they broke in the July heat, they seemed to hide or suggest (did I know which?) the wavering angles of old and submerged walls. Everybody here was kind to me. I was the younger son and not a hired man. Yet Rafe was right; I should never be content, as he and Thorkell were, to spend my life tending a piece of land. I loved the maythe for its colour, the berries for the way that they nested, red-breast fashion, up in an old hedge; but both the new and the old were in me and I could not choose between them, so that eventually I should find no place at any man's hearth.

Without thinking, I had come back to the road that we had taken that first morning to Nansvean. The stream tumbled out of the woods, twisting among the rocks. It wakened me in the morning; I heard it speaking as I fell asleep at night. Mellyn, mellin—it was Cornish-sounding water; for mellyn in Cornish meant a mill, and mellin, yellow. They met and mingled again, the words, wherever light scampered on this hot yellow day. They tapped on the stones, waiting for a wind to start the wheel. Mellyn, mellin, yellow summer, yellow mill, there they were, bird-footed worts painted them along the inch-high grasses, repeated them again in the tall centres of the daisies. There was no land as beautiful as this. Bees were out, stones were warm as I touched them; how stupid it was to dream that any adventure offered more to me than this field! Rafe, Laurel and I would stay together in the valley, and once the ordinary pattern of our lives had ended, all that I would ask would be that something of this meadow's glory had coloured our simple lives.

The yellow mill. . . . Looking up at it this hot afternoon, words began to form in my head, not in the set pattern that Leofwen would have used, but haphazardly, as if they wanted to follow the splashing of the stream.

> *Mellyn, mellin,*
> *I saw you first*
> *by the mumbling water;*
> *a rake was lying*

58

on the thirsty coltsfeet
and the hay was in.

If Laurel came round this corner now on her way down
to the sea (and I thought of Egwin's words), should I
dare to repeat my song to her? If Rafe were not with us,
I was silent and shy. Of course I loved her, but I loved
Rafe too. Was he not the comrade who had rescued me
from Normandy? Only he did not understand her gifts;
he was almost afraid of them. "It's very beautiful, but my
mother always wore blue; I prefer blue," he had muttered
awkwardly when Laurel had shown him a stuff so like
the transparent feathers of the great butterflies about
Trewoon that I had spent hours wondering how she
could possibly have turned rough linen into wings. No,
he loved her; but she needed more than his loyalty. Kindness such as hers needed imagination to respond to it. I
remembered a moment when she had found me staring
at the autumn mist. "None of us wants winter," she had
said, "but look at those leaves! If they have to die, they
are offering us a banner against darkness. Their gold is
free, not locked up in a chest. We can learn so much from
them, Wulf, though not all lessons are easy. Summer will
come again, and while we are waiting for it you must
tell us more of Leofwen's stories."

I had been unable to answer her for a moment. It had
meant so much to me, for she did not like the tales herself; though whether this was because they were really
too wild for her or because of the Abbot's disapproval,
I could never discover. Then, this very spring, one Sunday afternoon, the three of us had gone down to a pool
below Nansvean, where somebody had once tipped a
broken cider press into the water. The reeds had grown

over it, and it was a favourite place for vivid green, inquisitive frogs. Without thinking, I had plunged my hand in to rub away the silt and feel the old stone rim under my fingers. "Oh, Wulf, let them alone," Laurel had cried from the bank as the frogs had hopped away to the supposed safety of a broad, neighbouring leaf. "I love the way they look as if they had on green coats of mail; splashing the water like that disturbs their freedom." I suppose the words had reminded me of Yorkshire, and I had said, drying my hand on a tuft of warm grass, "This summer I ought to go home." "Go home!" She had laughed at me as if I were six. "Hasn't Estrith been feeding you properly?" I had watched the frogs creep cautiously back to their cider press shelter, and answered, "You know when the time comes you will have to chase me from Nansvean yourself. I shall never leave you."

So many dog-roses had opened on the bushes around the mill that, though wild, they made the meadow seem a garden. The day grew hotter; the scent of the grasses made me drowsy. "If you want to sleep," a voice said above me, "it will be much cooler on the sands."

I looked up. Laurel was standing on the stone step of the stile that divided the upper from the lower field. "Where are your wits? Fancy sleeping upright on a bank in the full sun! Rafe told me that he had sent you off to bathe an hour ago. I expected to find you on the beach."

"Is he coming too?" I asked.

"Not today; I left him talking to a farmer. One of them, I'm not sure which, wanted to sell the other an ox."

"Rafe is taking the farm very seriously this season," I said as we walked on, side by side, across the maythe towards the cliffs. "We all have to grow up," Laurel murmured; and I thought she was serious till I caught her eyes and we both laughed.

"The mind was meant to fly, not always to tramp along a furrow, thinking the same thoughts, at exactly the same pace."

Laurel smiled again and I knew that she understood me. "What colour," she added softly as we climbed to the top of the last bank and stood with the sea below us and a ripple of foam even on this silent day beating against the rocks. "And the light," I said, "like all of us is a hunter. Look, it's out with a silver net to catch the tide, but the tide is slipping away from it back to deep water. Hurry, this is the best moment of the day if we want to swim."

Rosmellyn was usually deserted because there was no anchorage for boats. Cliffs rose steeply at either end of the half-circle of shingle. Gulls shrieked, and far off, on the rocks our sailors dreaded so much, a couple of black cormorants waited for fish.

We sat on the shore and let the sand drift through our fingers. Laurel was looking for shells. Some of them were shaped like miniature castles; others imitated the shallower pools. The fields were only a few feet above us, but what a different world this was from the land! Even when dry the seaweed was more like a stone than a plant, and though the pebbles under the water were as vivid as the butterflies, they had no wings. It was so hot that the waves seemed to move too slowly, coming towards us with the tide in long, fluttering lines that dissolved along the shore without leaving a mark. "This is paradise," I murmured, as the sun beat down on us; "if only it were always summer."

"We should soon get tired of it," Laurel answered, without much conviction.

"Why should we? People only tell us this because they are afraid to be happy. They want to impose their wishes on us, but why can't we be as we are? Let Egwin have his ale, Rafe his earth, and you the many colours of the ever changing sea. . . ."

"And what do you want?" Laurel asked, tossing a broken bit of cockle into the pool beside us.

"You," I said boldly, and nobody was more surprised than myself. I had always imagined that if Fate were to offer me a wish, I should choose knowledge or the power to wander through unknown cities. Now in this overwhelming moment I knew that for all his jesting Rafe was right. I loved Laurel. I wanted her more even than freedom.

"Flatterer," she teased, not taking me seriously; "how tired you would get of me."

"I mean it," I said helplessly, dazed by this sudden recognition. My doubts and irritations of the last weeks were suddenly plain. Happiness was the herb, I thought, for which we were all waiting; then everything was possible, only it was hard to bear. The perfection of this hot afternoon, and Laurel so near me that I could see the foam drying on her sunburnt arms, became so intense that I almost wanted to shake it away as if I were a dog struggling up from the water. I tried to take Laurel's hand, but she brushed me aside and scrambled up as if she were unwilling to believe that anything deeper were involved than the banter of a moment. "Come, Wulf," she said, and she started towards the path; "the others will be wondering what has become of us."

We stood for a moment at the top of the cliff. "Is anywhere as beautiful as this," Laurel repeated, putting my own thoughts into words. We waited before we turned up the valley (it seemed a lifetime though it could only have been a moment), while the sun began to set and the sea deepened into a vast, free semicircle of pointed, running waves.

"July is the white month," I said as we walked along the lane through the gathering dusk. White lace, white shells, white stars, everything was white and silver or a transparent, almost dusty grey. The only colour was an occasional claw of honeysuckle running up the hedge, or the dog-roses on the bushes beside the mill. Laurel pulled one of them towards her. "Once I thought I had got a shade like this, but when the dye was fixed it was such a flat and ordinary cream that I threw it away. What I like most about you, Wulf, is that you never laugh at me for trying to make new colours." Mellyn, mellin, I murmured to myself, though I still dared not say the words aloud. The moment of creation was an instant only in the long day of our lives, over before we realized its presence, subduing us to its influence ever afterwards. "Perhaps some tones are fluid," I suggested, "and even the thought of holding them is an imprisonment?" Laurel shook her head. "Rafe thinks I am crazy," she answered, almost sadly; "he wants to keep everything as it was in his grandmother's time, except for his land."

The scent of the bedstraw reached us from the fields; I could hear the last bees. I stooped to kiss Laurel's head, and though she broke away from me it was gently and without reproof. Instead she picked a rose and gave it to me. "Here is your flower," she murmured; "now we must go home." I took it; our eyes met; again I felt as if a wave were breaking over me, that it was a repetition of something that had happened before. Then, although I had boasted that I was willing to grasp all of life in a moment, I answered without thinking, "But the dog-rose only lasts a day."

"Wulf, where are you?" Laurel pushed through a gap in the hedge and came towards me down the field. I looked up in surprise; she so seldom left Nansvean after sunset. Then I brushed the dirt from my hands because I had been pulling up some weeds, and went to meet her.

"Working again," she teased. "It's very late."

"No, I came here to look at the sea." In this just-before-darkness moment when our cove was flecked with points of oyster light, the water gave me a particular sense of freedom. "Only I saw a groundsel about to seed over the path so I pulled it up."

Laurel hesitated. I was silent. We must have stood for a full moment looking at each other. "Has anything happened?" I asked.

"I thought you would rather hear from me, Wulf, than from the others. My uncle is worse; sometimes I wonder if he will live to see the harvest he talks about so much. I am to marry Rafe next month."

It was what the village had expected for weeks, but this made the news no easier to bear.

"I should have liked another year," Laurel continued slowly; "one more July on our beach."

"Why must you hurry so? If the Duke wanted war

this summer, he would have sailed already." I quoted
Egwin in my misery though I knew that his reasoning was
false. "Do we have to believe every pedlar's tale?"

"This time it wasn't a pedlar. It was the Abbot. He
came today to advise us to marry at once because of
Penda."

"Penda!" I reached up and broke a twig savagely from
the hedge. "Why can't the Abbot complain to Bodmin?
Take your year."

Laurel shook her head. "The Abbot has promised his
protection to the farm if Rafe will take his counsel."

"And not join Harald?"

"He said nothing about the King. He pointed out that
if I am married during my uncle's lifetime, Penda has no
excuse to interfere. Otherwise he might say that Rafe
was a stranger who had seized the lands by force, and use
this as a pretext to attack us."

"And because they cannot control that plundering
brute, you are to be sacrificed!"

"Wulf, in a few months this will seem just summer
foolishness. Why, you know I have loved Rafe ever since
he landed."

"I did not know that you were serious," I answered
helplessly. Ours had seemed a timeless friendship, isolated
from the world, where a word was more than love and a
touch less than the apple branch we brushed in passing.
What had a pattern of children and household cares to
do with anything so innocent, so intangible? "I am the
one who knows your mind," I pleaded. "With me, you
would have your freedom."

"You feel that you are losing Rafe as well," Laurel
continued in deliberate misunderstanding. "Nothing need
change, I promise you, only you must be reasonable."

"Everything changes." We had always boasted that she caught our wishes out of the air and made them real to us. How could she be suddenly so insensitive? "Yesterday you would have understood," I told her miserably.

We faced each other in an awkward silence, and I heard Estrith's voice calling her, across the fields. It was suddenly dark and the shapes of the cows were shadowy as we turned towards the farm.

"Thorkell came today to ask if he could have you for the harvest. I do not want to feel that we are sending you away, but they need help badly at Trewoon."

"I am here to obey orders," I said stiffly.

"We shall never give you orders, Wulf; but suppose you join him tomorrow? In a few weeks this strange summer with its plagues and rumours will be over. Then you will come back to find the same Nansvean waiting for you. Why, Rafe wants to alter the big barn, and he says he can't begin without your help. When Easter comes again you will have forgotten this surprise. How can we ever be other than friends?"

"I will leave tomorrow as soon as it is light," I said; and then, I could not help the words coming, I added, "What did I tell you, Laurel, the dog-rose only lasts a day."

My songs left me. It was a dreadful August. I blamed Laurel; I was jealous of Rafe; then, in moments of an overpowering clarity, I realized it was my own fault that she still thought of me as a boy with spring fever. With all the landscape changing round us, how had I failed to notice that love, too, was altering from a surface beauty to a deep endurance? For many summers it had been enough to watch Laurel, sometimes to be with her or fetch her roots. It was only after we had stood together beside the mill that I had known how much more she meant to me than my own life.

Thorkell guessed what had happened and kept me busy in the fields. He was a silent man, a little like Rafe in his devotion to the farm, but without Rafe's vision. I followed the reapers, swearing to myself that I would return to Nansvean at dusk and make Laurel understand me. Then, as night fell, I would remember bitterly that I was landless and friendless, and that mere understanding of her wishes was an empty gift if the price of it were a ploughman's hut isolated in some waste of bracken.

Evening after evening, I sat under the apple tree with Thorkell, dazed with despair. There was an evil of time and place. The seasons followed each other with their interplay of sorrow and happiness, little events, the small, regular festivals. We imagined we knew the tricks of life as well as we knew those of a favourite hawk. Then Doom swung from an unseen corner; lives crumbled in a shorter time than it took darkness to obliterate a sunset; we woke up paralyzed and beaten men. There was no reason now why I should not find my way to Bodmin to join King Harald's army, but I lingered waiting for a message to come. Surely Laurel would send for me before it was too late?

More and more rumours, sometimes actual news, reached even Trewoon. It was said that the Godwin brothers were negotiating a truce and would divide England between them; but that, I knew, was not Harald's way. A Breton trader told us that the King of Norway had already sailed; then the Abbot heard that sickness had broken out among the ships and many vessels had anchored in a Scottish port. I noticed uneasily that nobody spoke of Duke William, then in my wretchedness let myself forget our peril. For the first time, now that even Estrith was talking about war, it seemed too remote to happen.

I was sitting outside the farm one evening, almost in a fever from remembering other, happier summers, when Thorkell came over from the stables. "Suppose you try a day's fishing tomorrow," he suggested. "I want to give the barley in the top field another two days."

"Can two days make any difference?" The monotonous labour of reaping, of feeling that once our winter food was stored I should be free to return to Nansvean, seemed easier than tossing in a boat and struggling with my thoughts.

"This year they can. The crops need whatever sun they can get. It will be the poorest yield that I have known since I began to farm. Besides, the men haven't stopped work for more than ten days; they need a rest."

"Where do you want to go?" I asked.

Thorkell hesitated. "I can't come with you myself. Master Rafe wants to see me about the harvest."

"Why hasn't he come to us?" In the three weeks since my arrival there had been no word from him.

"I expect he has had no time."

I dug the tip of my shoe suspiciously into the soft earth. This was a plot to separate me from Laurel, for up to now I had always been the messenger. "I think I will ride over with you too," I said. "I need my other coat."

"I can fetch you anything you need."

"By whose orders am I not to go to Nansvean?" I sprang up from the bench on which I was sitting with my fists clenched.

"Nobody has forbidden you to go to the farm," Thorkell answered quietly. "Only, I think it is wiser for you to stay here. Mistress Laurel has got enough to trouble her without your groans adding to her confusion. It would be a different matter if she did not love Master Rafe, but she does. We have all known this for years."

I shook my head. Neither Thorkell nor any man else knew of our day on the sands.

"As you know, Wulf, if there is no invasion I am moving to my own farm this Michaelmas. Ask Master Rafe to let you farm Trewoon for him. It's a wild place here and you love the moors."

"The day that there is no room for me at Nansvean, I am going back to Yorkshire."

"By next spring you can join the King's standard or sail in Leofric's ship. Till then you are needed here. We are all afraid of Penda. He and his men are now in the next valley, and there are less than a dozen of us able to bear arms. Between him and the Norwegians and the Normans I often wonder if I have not carried my last load of hay. I know that it is hard for you to wait, but at present we cannot spare you—for Mistress Laurel's sake, if you like. Do you understand?"

"I must go once to Nansvean." Laurel had to know that I was more than a lovesick boy.

"Very well, but not tomorrow. I have heard that they expect a messenger at the Priory. Let me go and get the news. It is only a day's delay."

There was a movement, a sliding noise in the bushes and I jumped. "No," Thorkell said, "that was an animal, not a man. Penda is waiting to see what happens, how many of us join the King. We have a few days yet, just the time of the harvest. Still, it's a bad sign to hear badgers so close to a barn. It means that food is already scarce in

69

the woods or else there is some disease." He prodded the stems with his stick, but now everything was silent again. Then he looked up, seemed about to speak, but hesitated. "What is it?" I asked wearily, for I had an overpowering desire to see Laurel even if it were only for a moment. "If you are so unhappy, Wulf," he looked round as if he felt that somebody might have followed us, "go and see Mistress Gwyneth. I have known her give people very good advice."

I stopped my pony at the top of the hill. If I disobeyed Thorkell and took the broad track down the valley, I should reach Nansvean in a couple of hours. Otherwise, any one of a dozen little paths would lead me eventually to that waste of heather, bees and solitary, ancient stones that we called the Moor.

I sat in the noon sunlight, wondering which road to choose. My future depends on what I do, I said to myself; and then I smiled. If Laurel really loved Rafe, what would it matter whether I turned to left or right? It would only make matters worse if I went to the farm and Laurel refused to be alone with me. Almost unconsciously, I took the reins and moved away, between high banks of fern. "You must look for a pool on the far side of the trees," Thorkell had said, "if you want to find Mistress Gwyneth."

No sunshine penetrated the lofty, tangled foliage, and even on this August day I seemed underground; it was dark, shadowy and damp. The surface was slippery and so narrow that the fowl I had bought that morning and tied behind my saddle, bumped against the bracken as we rounded the corners. I was curious about Gwyneth. The tales about her were so different; though they had this aspect in common—they were always coloured by the speaker's own views. To the Abbot she was a figure of evil. "I caught two men smearing honey on an oak," he had complained to Rafe. "It is all that old crone's fault, she ought to be hunted over the cliffs." Thorkell said that she had cured more coughs and wounds than Brother Thomas, and that she always knew when a cow was going to die, or how many bushels of corn he would bring to his barn. Of course she could not help me, mine was a different problem. Yet Thorkell, whom I respected, assured me that she was wise. "Listen to her, Wulf; she will tell you stories of the days when Cornwall was as full of kings as it now is of stones." Perhaps she was another Leofwen? Or an old woman to whom loveless maids brought their troubles. Even, as some whispered, the last daughter of the last prince of this land.

I had often boasted that I knew the land around Nansvean backwards, but this was an unknown track to me. At moments it almost disappeared, and I pushed on between the bushes, wondering if I had lost my way. Then the trees ended suddenly, and I rode out into full sunlight. Far away, it might have been five miles distant, a V-shaped cove of sea, the dark blue of a chief's collar, was just visible between great cliffs. Otherwise there was heather from end to end of the horizon, with a little pool below me, so full of watermint that I thought at first it was a garden.

No wonder people returned with strange stories! This was an old landscape; I could feel it watching me as I rode forward. My pony shied as an adder crawled slowly towards the stones of what appeared to be a deserted pit, near a little stream that trickled from the pool in the direction of the coast. By the time that I had reached the bottom of the hollow I was up to my saddlegirth in meadowsweet, the luminous whorls pressing together in a feather of bloom after my broken passage.

There was no sign of either hut or life. I dismounted and picked a stalk of watermint, glad to feel the sun on my arms after a damp, uncomfortable ride. Then I lingered a moment, with the fragrant, grey smell of the mints filling the air, wondering what to do next? If I tried to cross the pond the roots might trap my pony's hooves. Finally, further down, at the narrowest point of the stream, I discovered two stepping stones. I almost shouted for joy when I got to them; they were marked by the still-wet footprints of a medium-sized dog.

We followed the animal's tracks up the bank and over a meadow. At the top, sheltered from the wind by another clump of trees, I saw a cottage inside a wattle fence. It was a sentinel's post, so placed that a stranger might have missed it easily, looking across the cliffs towards the sea. I tied my pony to a ring near the gate, opened the latch and walked up the orchard. Mistress Gwyneth was sitting on a bench in front of a scented, yellow creeper. She was not in the least like the crone that I had expected, being tall, almost like Laurel would be if I could imagine Laurel as old and, as I came nearer, she smiled. "You have been a long time getting here," she called out gaily. "How is Master Thorkell? Anxious, I suppose, about his harvest?"

"It's a bad summer," I stammered. Every fool who passed must have used the same words but I was suddenly tongue-tied and stood there, pushing the fowl into her hands, like any awkward yokel.

Gwyneth shrugged her shoulders. "What did you expect after the comet? It was a warning, but you have forgotten how to read the skies."

"We always hope," I protested. "How could we go on ploughing if we knew that the seed was for the land only and not ourselves?"

"Hope? Yes, that is why you bring me mackerel and pats of butter. I will say that this is the fattest chicken I have seen since Master Thorkell rode over in the spring." She felt the breast with expert, sun-burnt fingers. "But in return I suppose you want fair words, that you will get the girl you fancy, or waggons brimming over with corn."

"I did not come for that," I replied angrily.

"No, you came because Master Thorkell sent you. How is he?"

"He is well. It is true that he suggested my riding over to see you, but it was already in my mind. I should have come a month ago, but there was so much to do."

"Less than usual because of the rain. No, you have been hanging about Nansvean, hoping Mistress Laurel would take you to Rosmellyn with her."

I looked up in astonishment. What had the farmer told her? Gwyneth put the fowl on a stool beside her and laughed. "It wasn't Master Thorkell," she assured me.

A wild hope raced through my mind. "Has Laurel been here herself?" I almost shouted.

"No." Gwyneth's voice was cold and bitter. "Laurel belongs to your new obedient world. Perhaps it is better. I am the last of my race, of the free glory of Cornwall."

The sharp features under the white hair reminded me of the rocks that guarded the entrance to our cove. She must be very old, I thought, and for the second time I felt that I was looking at Laurel. "You remind me of her," I murmured.

This seemed to please Gwyneth, and I felt her eyes on me, almost as if she were seeing me for the first time. "There will be no fair words for you about your girl," she said, pushing away a basket so that I could sit beside her on the bench. "It would have been better for her to marry you, but I doubt if it will happen."

I struggled not to listen to the words, and yet I knew today for the first time how vain it was to hope. Laurel did not love me. I wanted to go back to my pony, but my legs seemed incapable of movement.

"Better for her, worse for you, but you cannot understand this at the moment." I shook my head; I felt that I was pleading with her to unsay the words, as children cry to the harper that they want the captive to come back to his home, in the middle of a story.

Gwyneth patted my shoulder. "I am not going to let you bring me the best fowl I have seen since April and go away desolate. Will you wait here while I fetch some mead? My bees get their honey from a royal heather, and there is only one spot left where it grows. Then, although you are saying to yourself it is impossible, I may be able to help you."

"I will wait," I promised.

Gwyneth got up very slowly, but she stood as erect as a man. I had not expected her to be so tall. The long enveloping cloak that fell to the ground was a pattern that our grandmothers had worn and woven of undyed wool, but clean and without a hole. She patted my shoulder again as she passed. After all, I thought, stretching my legs in the sun, why should I believe what she says? She does not like Laurel. A love that can be influenced by foolish words is itself foolish. It would have been the same with Leofwen. He would never have wanted me to marry. The old forget, and all they want is peace.

This meadow was as rich as the fields below our mill, but it had a different fragrance, it was wilder. The grass stalks (and I licked one), had the flavour of wood rather than of salt. We were farther from the shore. The honey-scented creeper rambling above my head was in full flower. An old dog blinked his eyes at me silently and turned over in the sun. There were bunches of water-mint hanging from the eaves to dry in the heavy air. It hardly seemed a moment, though it must have taken her some time, before Gwyneth came back with two cups and a jar. Mead was never my favourite drink, it was too sweet; but as the first sip went down my throat I knew that this was a liquid I had never previously tasted. Gwyneth smiled as I choked. "This is Maldor's drink," I said in surprise. He was one of the old kings. "You told me it was mead."

"So it is, but properly made with the right herbs and . . ." she looked at me as if daring me to question her, "with the right words. To make mead there must be songs."

"So Leofwen said; he was a harper at my father's home. Women sing here as they make it. I have heard them, but their mead is not like this."

"They do not understand the words today, and they will not take the trouble with the bees. Now, who is your Leofwen? Master Thorkell has told me about him; he must have been one of my companions."

"I learned all I know from him," I answered, taking a second sip. It was as if I were back in our courtyard and he was lifting me up to see the apple trees; then I seemed to feel the pressure of his arms on that last, cruel night. "This is my punishment," I moaned, thinking about Laurel. "I ought to have left here five years ago and gone to him in Yorkshire."

"That is the last thing that he would have wanted you to do. According to Master Thorkell, he was at death's portal when you left him; and to have risked being sold again into slavery by some rogue of a captain on the chance that you might weep over his grave is simply a girl's foolishness. You have work to do. Work he gave you. When are you going to begin it?"

"Work to do?" I babbled stupidly.

"You know the tradition; perhaps you are the last generation able to sing our songs."

"I do what I can, but people are too busy to listen or they are afraid. . . ." Laurel often found an excuse to leave if I began even a harmless story.

"Yes, I know the Abbot tries to root them out; but even if he alters hearts, the landscape will remain. There will always be men who ache to know its secrets; but change is cruel and what dies, dies. The words have to be handed on."

"I know," I murmured, and I thought of the new art and Brother Thomas meditating over his blazoned, static flowers.

"I have often watched you wandering about the moors, though you were too lost in your own thoughts to notice me. Come to me whenever you like and I will teach you what I know, that is, if there is time. This summer I have been horribly afraid. . . ."

"Tell me what is going to happen," I begged. The mead was clouding my mind, but behind the scents, the butterflies and the grasses, I seemed to see Rollo on his horse, a sword lifted above his helmet and the weapon beginning to descend.

"It is the Doom," she said. Her eyes were so wild that in spite of my clouded head I wondered if her long isolation had driven her crazy. Then I shivered, for without willing it I felt that she could see my thoughts.

Gwyneth smiled. "You think I am mad," she continued. "No, these are simply words that your new world has taught you. People have forgotten the old virtues. They want ease, not axes."

"Cannot we have, both axes and—compassion?"

"You can, Wulf; you have your songs. Yes, you are too light to swing an axe." She looked at me sharply in spite of my strength. "I never said that there should be no lawgivers or scribes, though songs were meant to be taught by the old to the young; their virtue leaves them once they are written down. But the folk should be trained to war, ready to die for their liberty with their weapons in their hands."

"It was the old way," I agreed.

"There were men living on these moors long before the Great Snow drove our forefathers to England. They have left a painting on a stone near Trewoon. I have often wondered what the words mean below it, but they are broken and in another language. Besides, when has reading brought anything but harm to us? Then these men grew tired. They forgot how to sleep in the open among the gorse or how to handle an axe. We were winterhardened, and those we did not kill jumped from the cliffs or fled into the hills."

"I was thinking about them as I rode to you."

"And before them were others, always others; even

77

the sea has forgotten its beginning, and no skies speak to us plainly. At your age, naturally, you think only of your own birth and death, but to me it is the folk that matters. First we were young and conquerors, then prudent and peaceful; now the death urge has come, and it is not within the power of any Earl, brave as he may be, to save us."

I bent my head, for she was telling me my own belief.

"It is not pleasing—as you come from Nansvean I will not say to the gods, but to Fate—when men ask other men to choose their rulers and to fight their battles for them."

"Yes, that is what the village says, 'It is only a shift of lords, nothing will change,' till I cannot talk to them any longer."

"All of us are infected, even you. Suppose I asked you to stab Ethelred, that fat, Norman-loving neighbour of yours, in his sleep, would you do it?"

I shook my head. "I will go to battle gladly, but he would be an unarmed man."

Gwyneth laughed. "You see. Ethelred's sloth, and he is only one among thousands, may lose your liberty for you, and yet you will not harm him. How reasonable men are!"

"If I did," I protested stubbornly, "I should become like Penda."

"I am not asking you to touch Ethelred," Gwyneth continued thoughtfully, "but I want you to see that only the ravens will be happy. We cannot escape our Doom."

"If we held together . . ." I began.

"That people will never do; they are too selfish. And now, let us forget about wars and talk about you yourself. The sun will be setting in a few minutes, and you have a long ride home." She leaned over and refilled my cup.

I leaned back against the wall, sipped the golden liquid and stared across the moor; the dog slept; the scent of the honeysuckle mingled with the mead, till the peace of the place obliterated my unhappiness. Even when Gwyneth began to speak, it was the remote sea that I heard rather than her words.

"You came to me for advice, Wulf, and how can I help you? I have watched Laurel since she was a child clutching Rafe's hand; and I cannot tell you that you will live happily with her, because it is she who has chosen and not you."

"I love Laurel," I murmured involuntarily.

"I know you do, but we cannot always have what we wish. No, I doubt if you will stay in Cornwall, but I think in some ways you will be happy. After all . . . ," she looked towards the old rocks covered with lichen lying in the heather, "you are simply repeating the history of your forefathers. They fled here from the ice; perhaps you will carry their traditions to a second, less weary earth. Yes, you will take your loyalty, Harald's homage, after many have forgotten him, to another lonely land. And now, whenever things seem harsh, remember that there is neither ploughing nor loving in war. If you have to join the King's banner, it will be easier to march without a girl crying out to you. This is England's year and not your own."

"Yes," I answered, and I thought of Rafe with pity for the first time for many weeks.

"Now you must return to Trewoon, but if I am here in the winter . . ." She stopped, and I noticed anxiously how frail and cold the hands were, lying in her lap. For a second I wondered if she were going to ask me to stay with her? Then she drank a little of the mead from the almost untasted cup beside her, and continued more firmly. "Come over to me and I will finish what your Leofwen began. You still have much to learn."

The clouds, the dying day, were full of turbulence and shadows as if the battles had begun already in the realms of the dead. "And afterwards?" I asked. Was it nothingness, a sleep, as they said, upon a frozen wave, or was there some final peace?

"No man knows," Gwyneth answered, "but the warriors are happy. I am sure each wins his crown, though your Priory friends would hurl me over the cliffs for saying so. What hostage can you give for courage? Our last battle has to be faced alone."

"All I should like to know is, why are we so cruel?" I thought of the Abbot's scorn of this suffering face above me. ". . . not in combat but in our own hearts?"

Gwyneth did not reply. The sun had set, and I stood up. I took the chain that Leofwen had given me and would have hung it round her neck, but she pushed it away. "No," she said, "that is something that you must not give, even to the girl you love. Greet Master Thorkell and tell him I should like to see him again. If he asks you what I have advised, say that I want you to be patient this year but he is to let you wander with the spring." She led the way to the gate, but as I unhitched my horse she pointed to the moors. "Royal heather," she murmured, "Arthur's heather. Remember your inheritance whether you go or stay."

A final ray of light fell on the wattles. Gwyneth's head shone in it as clearly as if it had been noon. For a moment I seemed to see Laurel's face under the wrinkled skin; then the light vanished and she was simply an old woman, eager for a little food. I tried to thank her once more but she waved me off. "Follow the stream for about a quarter of a mile and you will find a much drier path back to Trewoon." My pony moved impatiently forward. We splashed across the water; when I turned, Gwyneth had gone and there was only a solitary hut hidden among the trees.

Thorkell was waiting in the yard for me. "I expected you an hour ago," he said reproachfully as I dismounted. I was full of my adventure, but he did not ask me where I had been, so I walked sulkily over to the stables. He had sent me himself to see Gwyneth, and I resented being rated like a boy who had failed to come back quickly after some little, neighbourly errand.

Thorkell saw that he had hurt me, and he followed me to the stall. "I'm sorry, Wulf; I was impatient, but there is news. The King of Norway has sailed; Tostig is with him and our army is marching north. We are to defend the South."

Now that the actual warning had come, all I could think of was our uncut barley. "And the harvest?" I said anxiously. "There is barely enough for the winter if we gather in every stalk."

"We have five days. All of us agreed that we must get the crops in first."

"And Penda?" What was to prevent him from seizing the farms once the armed men had left?

"Even Penda dare not touch lands belonging to the King's soldiers. Besides, his men smelt plunder and half of them left him yesterday. Our messenger was told that

Penda had sent word he had an ague and would follow later. Others say in the village that he fought to prevent the band from leaving and was wounded in the leg. I think myself he is waiting to see which side will win."

I went on rubbing a wet strap vigorously that was spattered with mud from my ride. Penda's men would not be easy comrades, and I wondered if we should begin the muster with a battle among ourselves? Thorkell must have guessed my thoughts for he added quickly, "The meeting place is Southampton. Rafe is sending Leofric to Porthowel tomorrow to try to find us places on a ship."

"A ship!" I said in admiration. Rafe was a good leader. None of our neighbours would have thought of it, and it would save us from a fortnight's marching and probably many quarrels. "But do you think he will find one, so late in the summer?"

"He may. The seasons seem to have changed places this year. We are having the weather now that we ought to have had in June. But leave those reins and come and eat. We all have to be in the fields as soon as it is light; and while you are having supper tell me about Mistress Gwyneth. I hope she was kind to you."

It was later, after we had finished our meal and I had repeated something, though not all, of what Gwyneth had said to me, that Thorkell put his hand on my shoulder. "It happened today," he said, "as soon as the messenger had gone. Rafe married Laurel in the Priory Chapel."

"Married!" I sprang to my feet. "What treachery!"

"No, Wulf, it was not treachery. Rafe told me to ride here and fetch you over, but I refused. Mistress Laurel has sadness enough in front of her without your reproaches."

"You knew last night, yet you promised that I should see her again."

"What did Mistress Gwyneth tell you? It was Mistress Laurel's choice, not yours."

"That I will never believe," and I thought in anguish of the feel of her hair as we had stood together below the mill. "If I had seen her again it would never have happened."

Thorkell did not answer, and for the second time in my life my world was shattered. No matter what memory came to me, it only made my loss the more profound. If I thought of the sea I saw myself standing in the ship beside Rafe. Nansvean was all Laurel. Gone, gone; everything had gone. I almost laughed aloud under this dark and sultry sky where only the evening before I had wondered whether the scent of the bee blossoms was possibly that of the stars. Now all that I dared remember was Rollo. Perhaps he was riding across his drawbridge at this very moment, Eudo behind him, almost hidden in the folds of the heavy black and scarlet banner. "The Normans have been waiting for the King to move," I said, and I felt Thorkell stiffen. "You are right, nothing matters, our destiny is upon us."

I could never remember the details of the following days. We worked from dawn until it was too late to see, getting in the remnants of the barley. It was a full month later than any harvest that I remembered. Two days after the wedding, as we were cutting the next to the last row, I saw Egwin coming up the field.

"There is bad news," Thorkell said. "Look at his

solemn face, though I often wonder if that fellow doesn't enjoy making people unhappy?"

A dozen black crows clattered angrily out of the furrows as we tramped along the side of the hedge to meet him. I think we both knew what Egwin had come to tell us, that Laurel's uncle was dead. "He's gone," Egwin bellowed as soon as he came within hailing distance, "last night, in his sleep." Then he added with an air of vindictive triumph, as he came nearer, "The rich and the poor, they all meet in the same earth. Yesterday he was sitting in his carved chair to watch the women milk; and what use are all his cows to him today?"

"He lived a good life," I answered indignantly. I could have slapped Egwin's face for his insinuation that the old thane had ever been miserly or proud. "He was always kind; there was food for everyone who needed it; he helped the stranger. . . ." Then I stopped, for I saw Egwin looking at me with a sneer. In a time of plenty the villagers forgot easily that neither Rafe nor I were of Cornish birth, but now that war was near, we were to blame for the muster, the bad crops, even for the weather!

"And Mistress Laurel?" Thorkell asked hastily, to prevent a quarrel.

"She sent me to give you the news and to tell you not to come over for the funeral. Fighting men are to meet at Nansvean courtyard three mornings from now, and she says you will have enough to do here to get ready in time."

Thorkell nodded gravely. He showed no emotion, but he had been the old thane's man and I could feel his deep distress. "How many men are going from the village?" he asked.

"Three, and four from the farm. Seven too many from

this small valley. It is a question for the thanes, not us. What does it matter who is our King? The taxes will be the same at the finish." "The Duke will double them," I began, but I felt Thorkell's restraining hand on my shoulder and was silent. "And what are you going to do all winter? I would have joined you myself if it had been spring," Egwin continued almost piously, "but who is going to freeze in a watch tower all December on bad fish and a crust of mouldy bread?"

"The King sent us our orders," Thorkell answered simply. "Tell Master Rafe we shall be there." I marvelled at his loyalty, for I knew that Thorkell, too, felt that no fleet would sail before the spring; and he was leaving not only Trewoon but his own new farm. I saw him glance up at the reaped fields that were now the colour of a withered rose, and then he said almost sharply, "Will you finish the last row for me, Wulf, while I take Egwin up to the house for some food? I will bring the waggon with me when I come back. There is no time to lose."

The old thane was not alone in his death. "One disaster leads to another," as Estrith was fond of saying, shaking her head and twisting her apron up between her fingers. They came to fetch Thorkell to Mistress Gwyneth, the day before we were to march. A fisherman from the hamlet on the cliff had found her dead on the rushes just inside her door. We could not both be spared, and Thorkell was her kin. "It was merciful," he said, as I helped him saddle his horse. "I could protect her as long as I was here, but she had many enemies." Then he added as an afterthought, "How the animals and the moor people loved her!"

I worked till dusk. Then I went to the line of trees above Trewoon, to wait for Thorkell's return. How old the trunks were! Looking up at the ivy and the silver bark, I wondered if it were true that one of the last battles between the Bretons and my Saxon ancestors had happened on this very heath? They had fought us fairly and bravely; we had driven them brutally into the sea; was it their turn now to be avenged? What fever had they handed on throughout six centuries to weaken us now and make a newer, tougher folk without such memories, better fighters than ourselves? No thread was completely lost. "This is not your grandfather's England," Rafe had once said to me, up in the long field, "nor will it be your grandson's, but something in it will be common to you all."

Only this lonely ground seemed full of foreboding and expiation. Our life, our obscure village, depended upon two armies hundreds of miles away. We had to defeat both Tostig and the Duke or perish in what Leofwen had once called, "the dark ages of the old invasions." Nothing would escape them if they won, neither ships nor songs nor even the way we loved. Who would speak again of Gwyneth's princes except in an outlaw's hut in some dark fen, and for how many generations? Yet we seemed to be moving through some drama with our parts already assigned. No action could be changed; we were defeated in the sky before the shield wall formed itself on earth. It was so shadowy that I started. Was that a young face in an old helmet in the oval of the leaves, on guard, waiting, knowing that the last boat had sailed, and that he would never see the tiny, spotted eggs in the nest under the apple trees or hear the gulls again? There was a trampling of hooves; an axe clang on stone; I shivered, too frightened to turn. Then I caught the flash of a buckle, and Thorkell rode back hurriedly, bare-headed and stern. "We buried her on the moor," he said, "just as she would have wished."

THE COLD WIND or the rolling of the ship woke me before dawn. I was lying at the stern, under a pile of fleeces that a sailor had lent me. Our oars were shipped and we scudded under sail, in a short, disagreeable, duck-like waddle. Looking up at the dark sky, I envied the gulls, flying straight to harbour.

I was not sea-sick, but I could not rest. The preparations were over and here we lay, on a hard deck, with nothing to do but think. We had mended and polished, got new cloaks, adjusted every link and buckle of our armour, not for a Michaelmas of goose and apples but to go into the shield wall, to hack or be hacked to pieces. We had joked for years about Rafe's cap. "Keep away from that helmet, you'll scratch the steel." Now it swung from a rope in front of me, half full of bread for the journey. I should never have gone out fishing in a new leather coat—and mine had metal rings on the shoulders—but in war nothing mattered; prudence was an empty word; we lived completely in, and for, the moment.

It was five days since we had left Nansvean. I had slipped away at dawn without saying good-bye. There had been so much to do, collecting the men, the horses and the food, that it was only when Thorkell had said, half-way across the moor, "I was sorry I couldn't move that cherry tree, Master Wulf, but there wasn't time," that I had realized we rode, perhaps for the last time, across Cornwall. I had even forgotten to stop to wave to Estrith from the chicory patch as we always did when we went out hunting. Three flowers, so blue that I often imagined them to be square tatters of sky, grew on a sunny bank.

Rafe had caught up with us at midday. Thorkell had offered him wine; I had taken his horse. I remember knotting the reins in my hand with a feeling of relief that I had not had to leave the yard with Laurel's eyes watching me, and, underneath this, shame to feel such relief; and from another, deeper layer of being—so that my whole self became a battlefield—I wished that Laurel were mine and mine only, whether I came back or not. After a short rest we had started again. It was one of those warm, end-of-summer noons when cattle seem to chop at grass as if by chewing against time they could keep off winter, but the familiar landmarks were cold. Ivy on a stone wall, the long bramble broken with its own blackberries, my eyes had seen that these were beautiful, not my heart. "Thorkell couldn't move the cherry," I had said, "the one with the waterlogged roots too near the stream; perhaps we could risk it February. . . ." Then we had both smiled uneasily, realizing that we marched with our old-fashioned axes against horsemen, each a small castle in himself; and I had been furious for the rest of the day because I had reminded Rafe of the farm. "It is easier for the Normans," Rafe had said later, as we trotted over the matted, unending moor; "they grow up among spears, not trees."

Two days out, just in front of the harbour, a short

figure had sprung wildly into the road. "It's Leofric," I had said, recognizing his round fur cap with the bare patch behind from leaning continually against a wall. "I've found a ship, I've found a ship," he had yelled, jumping up and down like a child in front of a woodpecker's nest. "Nobody has ever seen such a boat. It's got a mast. . . ." And his arms had shot wildly above his head as if that gesture would convince us of its majesty. "Is it a galley?" Rafe had asked. "Yes, with double the Seagull's oars," (the Seagull was the vessel in which he sailed annually to Armorica), "and quite new cordage. Oh, I was frightened," his words had run together in his excitement, "she sails tomorrow for Southampton, and I did not know when you would come. They said this was the only road and I have been waiting and watching since noon, but there might have been another path; I haven't been easy a moment. . . ." Looking down I had seen a collection of whittled sticks and a wine skin at the bottom of the bank, so Leofric had toasted our departure, whatever else had happened. "We shall have to find out first whether the owner will take us," Rafe had replied, looking relieved, "and what it will cost."

Surprisingly, Leofric had been right. I had never seen so large nor so splendid a ship, with wide beautiful sails of that tawny colour they paint lions in the bestiaries. The captain was thin and dark, ignorant of our tongue, but a sailor like Leofric. Both felt for the wind in the same way, and talked endlessly about the weather in a mixture of grunts and signs. It had not been the captain who had bargained with Rafe but a small fellow, talking fluent, though a foreign-sounding, Saxon, who had greeted us on the poop. His name, he had told us, was Latif, but whether he were the owner or simply a merchant turned interpreter, we had not discovered. From the distance we had taken him for a youth, but face to face he was almost an old man, with agate eyes in a wind-burnt face. He had pulled a great hood over his head although it was not really cold, and a number of tiny bags swung from his girdle.

Latif had agreed to a surprisingly low price for our journey at once. "He likes the Normans as little as we do," Rafe had whispered after we had handed over the fare and walked away. "Probably they plundered him of his goods somewhere." I had nodded, tying up the laces of the little hide-bag where we kept our coins. In King Egbert's time the roads had been safe; people had taken their children on pilgrimages, and a great-grandfather of mine had brought a silver cup back safely from lands beyond Rome. Now it was unsafe to ride twenty miles without weapons. "Perhaps," I had said, thinking of the comet, "this is the end of the world."

"A world," Rafe had answered, "not the world; they have been saying that for centuries." He had left me then to go forward and arrange about sending the horses back to Nansvean (there would be little fodder in the wake of a great army, and we should be more independent afoot), while I had moaned to myself, counting and stacking our loaves of bread, that it was unpleasant to have any age crack about the ears, however much it might interest the chroniclers afterwards.

Both my other voyages swayed up and down before me now as we rose and sank in the trough of the waves. Lying on my fleeces, with the salt crust splitting from the breakers that the Northmen called *hrim*, I thought for the first time in years of my departure from Yorkshire. There had been a number of us hostages standing in a half-circle at the bottom of the cliff where the Danes quarrelled among the great raven-beaked galleys drawn up on the sands. We had waited for hours, lashed with cold that rebounded from the rocks while the raiders shrieked and drank and played ball with rings that represented a year's crop, so that much of the ransom money spilt over the shingle. All of us knew what harvests cost in toil, following the plough in bitter wind and sun; and here were the wages, meant to go back into our land, sucked greedily under by the sterile beaches. My companions had stared impassively at the sky, but waste had always sickened me, and when two gold coins rolled almost to my feet, I darted from my place to pick them up and slip them into my belt. The hostage next me would have knocked me down if I had not been a child, for we were supposed to show no emotion before the enemy. Yet my impulse had been a sound one after all, because years later it had been these very coins that I had given to Rafe to pay our passage back to Cornwall.

Fool that I was then, I had even been pleased when a young Norman, Rollo, had come striding through the wrestling, shouting Danes, to look at us. He had seemed, to my inexperienced eyes, so clean, so aloof, so much more civilized, in his flawless hauberk, than the raiders. He had wanted to take the youth next to me, but the boy had refused, in a mixture of head shaking and words, to leave his original captor. Rollo had shrugged his shoulders, had said something to the Danish captain beside him after glancing along our line, and tapped my arm. It was only after I had learned the Norman language that I found that for all practical purposes I had forfeited my hostage rights by following him obediently. At that moment all I had wanted was to escape from the Danes.

Yes, that first voyage had been a blank horror of sea-sickness and despair. Only a few impressions remained—the slow glide into a fortified Norman harbour, the broad, scarred hands of a rower handing me down my bundle when we were ordered into the row-boat to go ashore. Yet, and this was strange, for it was contrary to what our elders taught us, I had not had enough imagination to realize, and this was fortunate, how much worse than anticipation life under the Normans would prove to be. If I had, I should have leapt into the Channel at once.

The second journey! Ah, that was different. I could remember every minute of it, from the wild excitement as we pushed off from the sands to the relief, though our craft rode down a wave seemingly straight on its head, that we were free, as Rafe had jokingly remarked, to ride the furrows of the ocean. I know that he woke me with a laugh on the last morning, to point out green patches on the blunt rocks and smoke rising from a chimney, Nans-vean, though then we had not known its name. Even now I seemed to smell (was it fantasy or a breeze from the land?) the aromatic scents of the cliff-growing herbs.

Mellyn, mellin,

the song buzzed in my ears, then the Present, that run-away, that assassin, struck from behind into my heart. Oh, Laurel, I thought, Laurel, why did you have to leave me?

It was not only Laurel whom I had lost, but Rafe too. Even Cornwall. I looked up at the sky that spread from faint blue to dark and saw, instead of ropes and canvas, only the speedwell on that rock, the bird-wing blue, the white, the amethyst her cloak had brushed as she came over the stile. Everything reminded me of Laurel, and yet—if she were to come again, down the same path at the same hour of the morning, there would be a rift, an insecurity, a knowledge deeper than love itself, that a stone once cracked cannot be mended with words, that there is finality, that on that July evening something between us had forever ended.

It was only now, with the wind whistling through our steel caps hanging from the rigging, that I knew all that I had lost. Oh, not simply a girl, but the colour in all I did; yes, it was a dog's world now. Old poachers said there was no difference in a hound's eyes between the rust of a kicked-away bolt and the red rose. At Nansvean, Laurel's words had eased the despair of those final days, saved me, perhaps from myself. Suppose she had loved me, could I have borne to leave upon what I felt so deeply was a foredoomed adventure? All of us had ridden unwillingly from home towards a destruction we had never willed, forced upon us by some Fate outside our imagination. If I had hidden in the woods and crept back when the others had gone, what would she have said to me? Had she not spared me a choice I might have been unable to make, to go to almost certain death, abandoning her to nearly as certain danger?

I could not sleep. I could not lie another moment restlessly on the deck. My covers dropped as I sprang up to cross to the dipping, rising bulwarks. Why not dive—in a few moments it would be over. As a child, I had innocently believed Leofwen's words. I was to remember and teach his songs, to make some of my own. Now I knew that the greatest rune was no charm against battle, against love. Why not leap and break the endless round of captivity and sorrow? I leaned forward a little; the breakers were as shadowy and broken as my dreams.

Then the wind, no, it was somebody's hand, plucked my sleeve.

"Up so early?" Latif stood beside me, muffled up in an enormous cloak that turned him into a beehive.

"I was thinking that it was as hard to see the bottom of the Channel as to know who will reign over England."

"So you think William has a chance?" Latif looked at me searchingly. "Most Saxons laugh at him."

"Most Saxons have not been three years captive in a Norman castle."

"So that was it?" Latif stooped and pulled some fleeces into a seat beside the bulwark. "Sit down and tell me about it. If you can't sleep morning in, talk; it is much healthier than brooding about the future."

Sometimes a scene, unimportant in itself, is stamped on the mind as if time had drained out of it; and it hung, an arras, behind memory. So it was with this dawn. Every line of the planks, every fold in the canvas, the blue sky over the steerer's cap just a little darker than his tassels, were to haunt me for years. Latif's words, so much more worth remembering, vanished like foam. I saved a sentence or two; but others, the ones I wanted so eagerly to hear again, went beyond recovery.

"It's not the Normans themselves," I said. "I am even indifferent to them. It is what they do. Life is always hard, but they destroy everything that makes it bearable. What they call discipline is merely a form of slavery. The men are taken from the land and turned into soldiers to blight an ever wider radius of earth. Then their leader rides through villages of terrified, less-than-human serfs, and calls it victory."

I had seen Rollo slice all the hedge roses away with his knife as he rode along the lane merely because they were beautiful; and who, even among his priests, knew the meaning of compassion?

Latif nodded. He put his hand into one of his many little bags and pulled out a lump of rose-coloured, translucent sweetmeat. It stuck to the tongue with an unfathomable taste of burnt honey and something unknown, almost as of pounded flowers, quite different from the green, cool flavour of our herbs. Did its essence or its newness evoke dreams? As Latif spoke, I saw a rose-shaped city of white towers. (Who of my folk had been there? Yet I seemed to know the way, climbing step by step to the gate of the merchant's house.) Why, if I put my hands out I should feel the sweet, flat water that had no salt in it, the tubs of warm trees! For a long time I said nothing, while the clouds overhead spun themselves into terraces. Then to Latif, a complete stranger, I told things that even Rafe did not know about Rodwen, the ford, my captivity, our escape. "They tricked me," I kept saying; "how was I to know that by following Rollo that day, I lost all chance of getting home?"

"Why didn't your companions, the other, older hostages, warn you to stay with the Danes?"

"Because they were glad. If all of us had refused to go, Rollo might have taken somebody by force."

"You see, it is not a race but Man himself." Latif divided another fragment of his paste between us. "Was no Norman ever kind to you?"

"One of the men knew we were trying to get away. He said nothing; he liked Rafe."

"You seem to enjoy my jelly." He handed me another lump. "How do you think it is made? I've seen men ride to the ends of the empire to bring back some of its spices, and others work a lifetime blending them into pastes. If one of the twenty ingredients happens to turn sour they throw the whole barrel away. All of us are sometimes cruel; even a Norman, at one moment or another, may be kind. You cannot cudgel men to goodness with a battle axe, Wulf; what we want to know is the cause of our actions, and even then. . . ," he seemed to be speaking to himself, "it is only a beginning."

"But the castles," I protested, "they are pure evil; they corrupt the men who live in them."

"On the Duke's coast there are no raiders."

I looked up sharply. I thought for a moment, we are trapped; he is sailing not to Southampton but to Normandy; then I saw Latif smile at me, and knew that, whatever he chose to say, his heart was with Harald.

"The sailors on this ship have had more experiences than your ploughboys, but what have they learned from them? Listen to them on shore; all that interests them is somebody's wine at a wretched little harbour tavern. If I talk to you will you listen, or will you prod me with that too-ready dagger of yours, just because I say something you prefer not to hear?"

For answer, I unstrapped it and laid it by his side. Latif stretched his legs comfortably out in front of him and put his own small knife and the sweetmeat bag on the deck. "I like the Normans, Wulf, even less than you do. They spoil my trade, and if the Duke wins, this will be my last voyage to England. What are spices and silks to a man living in a hall as draughty as a dungeon and full of smoke? Toys for a church, yes; but their bishops buy in Rome and not in Syria. They caught my nephew on their sands, and you can imagine what happened to him. He was about your age; it was just a summer ago; that is why I made this journey. He had been battling with a storm for days and was driven ashore, only to be killed when he believed he had reached safety. It was pure luck that one of the sailors escaped and came to me with the tale. I could not have helped him, but I keep feeling if I had been there it might not have happened. It was his first voyage alone and not on his own ship, though he had made seven with me. I wanted him to wait until this vessel was ready, but he was impatient. He felt youth was so temporary. I cannot tell; my intuition is not as sharp as it was; we all get old, but I think this is the last time your wretched fogs will bring on my ague."

"I know," I moaned; "I have watched war coming for years. Nobody would listen to me."

"If you had that grain more of wisdom that you still lack (what was it that you told me about losing a falcon through flying it before it was trained?) I should say, leave Harald to his housecarles and come to Micklegarth next spring."

"I can't do that. I have to fight as long as there is a chance; otherwise, what peace should I have afterwards?"

Latif nodded. "Yes, you are right. With your temperament, you can't leave your comrades. Anyhow, not to struggle against injustice is to tolerate it. Suppose though, by some miracle Harald wins; are you really going back to Nansvean?"

The grey waves in front of me broke into the irregular lines of the hills above our cove. "What else is there to do?"

"We all need friendship, a mutual companionship or love. Love can fuse the most opposite natures together, though perhaps not for very long. Unless you have one or the other, life dries up. I think it would end for you if you went back to Cornwall."

Even if what the fellow says is true, I thought, I can only face our immediate peril. For the first time, as if to taunt me, I was conscious of personal fear, the moment when a guard breaks and the opposing weapon slashes down, no wooden practice blade but a heavy sword. Suppose I were to return; no words, however wise, could extinguish the faint hope that Laurel might want me back.

"Is it too hard?" Latif asked.

"It is not very likely that I shall have to make the choice."

Latif fumbled in another bag and some coins spilled over the deck. I swept them up and handed them back; they were round and heavy, with an emperor's head stamped on either side. From the depth of the wallet he drew out a little ivory wrapped in a fragment of silk. He held this for a time without speaking; then he began to chatter about his home. "Byzantium we call it; that Micklegarth of yours has a barbaric sound; it is not a hall in a saga, all mead and oxhides, but a palace where even the sunlight is cloth of gold. We quarrel with our neighbours over a philosophical point too tenuous to write down, but we wear no daggers, call out no armies." He handed me the little figure; was it a goddess or a woman? I had never dreamed hands were capable of such carving, and as I stared at it I felt myself wandering again, up steps to a door hung with silk, not scraps such as we used for banners but a curtain half the size of a sail. I knew if I pushed it aside I should come into a court where water dripped from a dolphin's mouth into a basin of floating lilies. Beyond the sound of this water there was something that Latif wanted to say, not the ordinary words that I was hearing now but a suggestion, an idea he had intended for his nephew if the boy had not raced off so impatiently, seeing his uncle as an over-cautious, elderly man. Whatever it was, it meant a lot to Latif; and I, like the nephew, would not hear, swinging up and down between hatred and love, the invaders and Laurel.

"You would like the horses, Wulf; they train them in the desert and call them after the winds. They are not like your great Norman brutes, meant to carry a barrel of iron."

"Nor would they live in our storms."

"Feel this dagger. It looks like a toy and is strong enough to cut through that spar."

"You cannot tempt me, even with swords. If Harald wins, I shall go back to Trewoon and grow oats." Every stalk in the valley was a cluster of bells.

"Have you heard of the Varangian Guard?"

I nodded. A youth, but he was ambitious, had gone to them from Normandy; they were picked men, and life was easy, only they never came home.

"You might be ruler of a province, Wulf."

And be lonely, I thought, even if it were always summer. "What should I do with a province?" I asked. "If I have to be alone, let me stay with my songs." Whenever there had been death on the farm or a plague of flies in the orchards, Leofwen had reminded us of our ancestor, the first Saxon, who had drifted to us in a coracle and taught us to plough. It had to be a grave moment, and Leofwen was grave as he chanted; but I had loved it more than all the other chronicles, though the words were hard and old. Especially the opening, when I had seen as I listened a child as young as myself, peeping from a cave where he was always cold and always hungry towards the pits of sand, the rubble of grey pebbles where his tribe hauled a strange, golden cradle to the beach. They had learned to sow; they had learned to spin; to forge iron arrow-heads and honour the gods. Then, for some reason I had never understood, the king had drifted out to sea again on a great ship; it was not a burial though he was very, very old, but he was needed somewhere beyond the seas. I suppose that it was the sense of wonder I enjoyed, the hope that something equally mysterious could happen on our moors and free me from some fear. Old history, the distorted memory of a landing, people said now, almost apologetically, as if there could not have been a time when we had crawled about like wolves; but it was so deeply in our blood that Brother Thomas explained it as the visit of a shipwrecked Irish monk. He dared not denounce it as a pagan story. Only a child could inherit a myth; it was his ancestors whispering him a cradle song, strangers would have their own. If the Duke won, if I followed Latif, what would it be? A scrap of seaweed to show the tides that a girl had nailed to the wall, to be torn down when its colours faded and burnt with the winter rushes.

Latif sat watching me. Why was he so anxious that we should sail together? I could not resemble his nephew except in years, and must appear barbaric to him with my country manners and great sheepskin cloak. I had caught him smiling at it as we had come aboard. Perhaps he noticed that I was puzzled, for he took the little ivory from my hands and held it to the light. "If she were lost, there are no carvers today able to mould such features; and here I am, carrying her in my bag, risking her to winds, pirates, even the ordinary harbour robbers! For comfort perhaps, foolhardiness, a reminder that life is not always salt water and rotten biscuits. What do you want to know?"

"That is my price," I said at last, "an answer to some questions; but what can she or you or any man tell me? Of good and evil, why some men are selfless like Leofwen and my father, others as rapacious as Penda." I almost trembled as I said the name, for I had not got Rafe's confidence in the Abbot. Who would protect Laurel if none of us came home?

"You would ask something difficult." Latif shook his head, though it was what he had wanted me to say. "Who told you, born merchant of hard bargains, to make runes? Come with me to the Caspian (and that's a name you hear for the first time) and during the ride there I will teach you to read our books."

"In our battles there are few survivors," I answered stiffly, while the rigging swayed down and up again as our swords had swung to Rollo's command.

Latif went on wrapping up the tiny statue as if I had merely made a remark about the waves. If his fingers were darker than my own, what was it but wind-burn and exposure to the sun? I wanted him to talk, to tell me more about his nephew. Everything he said was different from our grumbling neighbours, but he was quiet for such a long time that I feared I had offended him. "Tell me," I begged, for I was afraid of wasting more of these precious moments, "why do so many Saxons believe the Duke to be a better man than the King? I have seen Normans chase their serfs like hares and fire whole hamlets to free a forest for the deer."

"People usually see merely what they want to believe. It is much easier to throw your responsibilities on to somebody else, to blame King or Church for your follies rather than admit your mistakes. Only a leader has to appear virtuous, in memory of the time, I suppose, when they say the gods ruled us. The Duke makes his laws in the name of righteousness; the word morality is always on his lips, and he backs it up with a powerful army, trained to sin by candle-light or, at least, unobserved! King Harald leaves his citizens to judge for themselves, and they hate it. If he drinks, if he loves, he does it openly; he warns them of dangers to come and possible disasters. His weakness is that he relies too much on an old tradition of loyalty, that his subjects should come to his banner of themselves, and not by command. Some do," and he smiled at me, "but how many are sitting by their fires waiting to join the winning side? It is much easier to resemble your namesake, Wulf, than to be a man. Have you ever noticed how terrified people are of vision or thought?"

I looked up, so completely astonished that Latif began to laugh. "How do you like your first lesson, Wulf? You cannot plough values into straight furrows. Truth is eternal, but the colours change. If you sack a town, something is lost no matter how magnificent a city rises from the ruins."

He meant, I supposed, that our world, Leofwen's teaching, were to be destroyed. "If a mace is going to smash what I believe, why should I want to come back?"

Latif shrugged his shoulders. "Look at it this way. You told me yourself that in Yorkshire on your neighbour's farm the son and grandson had been killed fighting the Danes; there was only the grandfather left. When a council of elders gets too old, they are willing to barter any future for a present peace. Your fleet should be watching the Straits; why is it back in harbour? Perhaps your race has grown tired? What you believe is valid, but it isn't an orchard of apple trees; it can survive geographical changes very well," and he pinched the fingers of my cloak playfully, as if by making me step out of it I should cease to be a Saxon. "You must go on with your comrades, I agree, because I was never foolish enough to believe that philosophy dispenses a man from fulfilling his ordinary duties; but let us imagine that you come along the quay one evening, I don't care whether laden with booty or as a fugitive. You might consent to a voyage then, let us say, just for the adventure?"

"Anyhow I'll remember your ship." If he were lonely, and it cheered Latif to dream that I might replace his lost nephew, why be cruel and refuse him bluntly? Besides, the suggestion set my blood tingling. What youth would reject a chance to see, what had Latif called it, By-zan-ti-um, if he could accept with honour? "You will never be a stay-at-home," Leofwen had muttered, carrying me back on his shoulder the day that I had tried to run away to York—I might have been four. He was the only one to understand when I had babbled, "It came over me, I had to go." The women had said that a cow had frightened me, or that my ball had rolled too far and I had forgotten my way, but it had been something much simpler, as direct as scent is to a dog. I had dropped my playthings and followed the impulse because otherwise I could not have gone on breathing. Oh, what had we brought with us in our migrations? The same instinct pushed its way now between Harald and Cornwall. I seemed to feel a violent sun upon my shoulders; the outlines of the port were hazy only because I had been so long away from it. In anticipation I was leaping up the steps of a southern wall I already knew. Yorkshire had never seemed familiar; in Nansvean I was still a stranger. Latif's language (he was murmuring something in it) sounded like long, slightly broken waves. The only constant value was this thirst of mine for liberty. "I want to know many more things," I begged. "Why does the hawk return to its master? Bred in captivity the bird may be, but why does it fly back, even if death comes sooner in the wilderness?"

"Perhaps we depend more upon our early training than we know." Latif bent over an obstinate knot in the laces of his bag. I should have cut it myself, but he worked quietly at the little strands with more patience than I possessed. "Isn't there always somebody to rescue us from the imaginary perils of our babyhood? With me it was an old waterman who lifted me up to pat the sails. I was four at the time, and some fool had told me they were clouds and would blow me away to the dolphins. The waterman showed me how if he touched the rudder we would swing round and see my home. I have often wondered since if that wasn't the start of my living in boats when my family wanted me to learn the alphabet? Some of us follow the patterns we are taught, and some of us, the wilder ones, are seekers. Then our fellow citizens throw us into the wilderness if they can. Haven't you noticed how lazy people are? They would rather fight a war than change a habit. Yes, it is hard for the discoverers; though I have sometimes wondered," his voice dropped as if he were speaking to himself, "if we do not choose our lives because of some purpose we seldom understand while we are living them."

No, I thought, I never chose that autumn day when the messenger came to our courtyard, nor those cruel winters in the Norman keep. Give me a way, a hope, to find out why things happen!

"There are many questions you haven't answered," I said, "and it's day, I shall have to leave you."

"I can tell you one thing only, but you will like it. After we are old and have looked so closely at the world that it becomes a pavement of the four seasons our fingers have been fitting together, and from so far that we are falcons seeing a miniature earth, one element remains and that is freedom. It is, if you wish, another word for life; for without it everything is sterile, search is useless, our days merely mortality."

It was as if something inside me deeper than anything I had ever known responded, and I was silent, hardly able to bear the intensity of the moment.

It must have been a long time afterwards that Latif handed me back my dagger with a smile that was almost his way of speaking. "Be very sure, Wulf, that it is freedom and not intolerance." Then Rafe came striding up the rolling deck towards us, and stood, clinging to the rail. I thought that he looked at us suspiciously as if he wondered what this stranger and I had found in common. Latif noticed it too, and made a place for him beside us on the fleeces. "I was telling your friend, if this wind holds we should reach Southampton in three days." "That would be good." Rafe looked relieved; it was both safe and essential to discuss the weather. "I want to get our marching over before the autumn breaks." He looked back at the white surge flecking the waves, and I knew what was in his mind; every breaker took us farther from the farm. Yet speed was an antidote to the restlessness that we felt; the sooner we joined the army, the quicker the war might be over. I suppose we all had an unreasonable hope that we should survive to go home.

"Come and eat now before it gets any rougher." Rafe hauled himself to his feet and went off down the deck with a good imitation of Leofric's shuffle. Latif took no notice when I got up to follow. He had again become the owner of the ship, courteous but indifferent. I suspected that to this side of him, passengers or cargo were simply ciphers in the entity of the voyage. It was impossible to walk steadily, and I lurched along, clinging to the rail. Some of the men lay with their cloaks over their heads, beyond thought of breakfast. We unpacked some food and handed it to a sailor; he had swung two pots above a charcoal pan in the well of the ship, sheltered from the wind. "Can you understand what the fellow says?" Rafe nodded towards the distant figure on the poop now so tightly wrapt in skins that he was transformed into a conical tower. "I can't. He mumbles."

I dreamed I was alone on a half familiar moor, caught under the shallow, inverted basket of the sky. I wanted to get away, but wherever I ran, wolves galloped from pits among the heather roots, their jaws open above threatening, white fangs. I clutched my knife-hilt, but it stuck; the more I tugged, the tighter it clung to the sheath. The first wolves melted past me into the mist, but others came and others; I looked helplessly up into wicked, triumphant eyes. Then a great brute sprang at my throat and I screamed. . . .

"Bad dreams," Rafe said as I sat upright and blinked. "They happen to us all before a fight, so don't go rolling them round into prophecies."

It was still dark. Thorkell was pushing some dry twigs under the iron pot that swung from stakes we had planted on the previous night. Somehow the glowing embers, as he stirred them, reminded me of Latif's coins; each charred stick as it flamed a final time carried a different picture to the ashes. When I looked round, I was not surprised at my nightmare. Most of the men were humped into distorted animal shapes under their heavy sheepskins or disguised by the bracken they had piled on themselves for shelter. Even their steel caps shone like ghostly hummocks near their heads.

I yawned. It hurt to move my cramped legs from the meagre warmth of my cloak. It was useless expecting me to fight (my brain whispered) before I had had my sleep out. I wanted to sink into unconsciousness, to be warm, forget . . . perhaps this was a nightmare, too, and I should wake in my attic at Nansvean, with breakers roaring viciously at the cliffs and the wind whistling between the stables. My eyes shut; yes, if I could stop this whipping cold across my shoulders, all might pass, everything might come right again. . . .

"You had better hurry if you want to eat." Rafe jerked my cloak away pitilessly. "We leave directly light comes." At that moment my sleepy eyes saw his face (Thorkell's twigs had flamed into miniature torches) and I knew that he had stayed on watch all night, dreaming of Laurel, no doubt, and not of wolves.

It was a bitterly cold dawn, so unlike the day that we had expected all summer. Doom's day, I said to myself, doom of us, doom of England. I eased my knife, but now that I was awake there was nothing wrong with it; it slipped in and out of the sheath as if waxed. Thorkell began to ladle broth into our cups, and a fellow beyond him sliced our last loaf into small pieces. The soup burnt my mouth, but the warmth of the cup brought life into my half frozen fingers. Nobody can be heroic at five o'clock of a cold October morning; and we huddled around the fire with green and queasy-looking cheeks.

108

It was barely a week since we had left Southampton, although we seemed to have been marching for a lifetime. Latif had found us a guide, Ulric, a pedlar's boy, who knew every footpath across the Weald. Otherwise, we should never have reached the downs, for the highways were blocked with riders from all over Wessex. Many, too many, of the men Harald needed so badly, lay dead or wounded among the villages. Few reeves had collected stores, in spite of the King's orders; so the farms along the main roads were rapidly stripped bare.

It was Rafe's Norman training that had saved us, I thought grimly, as I tried to make my morsels of bread last. This part of England was pitifully unused to war. We had kept to Rafe's original plan and refused the offer of horses. Instead, Ulric had led us along narrow fowling-tracks through the dense forest, taking more care to avoid our own thanes than any possible enemy. Occasionally a couple of us had walked into some isolated hamlet to buy food. Oh, what rascals the Wessex farmers were! They had charged us three and four times the market price, though we had left our own fields to go to their defence. Day in and day out I had heard men curse Rafe for making them crawl through thickets or scramble up the bare, exposed hills before it was light enough for herders to notice us, but now we were here, a few hours only from King Harald's camp, hungry, but without having lost a man.

Once I had rebelled myself. The day after our start, as we rested at noon, a horseman had galloped by in the direction of Southampton. "It's over," he had shouted in his soft South Saxon; "the war's finished. You can all go home." "Over!" Rafe had swung to his feet and caught the fellow's bridle as he stopped. "Then the Fleet was in the Channel after all; were many galleys sunk?" "The Fleet! What Fleet?" The man had looked at us suspiciously. "I mean the fight at Stamford. They say there isn't a Dane left worth a ransom." Then Leofric had run up with a wine skin; but the man knew no details, only that there had been great slaughter at a river near York, and that Harald was victorious. "Nobody can stand up to the King's axemen," he had yelled, wiping his mouth with his sleeve. "And the Normans?" I had ventured to ask as he held out his cup to be refilled. "The Normans. . . ." He had burst into wild laughter, for we were not the first that day to bid him drink to the King. "Why, how can they come through the gales? They are not even sailors. Next summer we shall have the housecarles here, and that Duke of theirs will think twice before risking his carcass on our beaches. No, the war is over; back you go to your ploughs." He had cantered unsteadily off, bellowing a song, while we translated the news to our men, most of whom knew only Cornish.

"I suppose it is true?" I had whispered to Rafe. The mention of York slung me into an agony of memory and guilt. Why had I lingered at Nansvean all summer? Because of Laurel, my conscience answered. I had allowed myself to discount reports of the King's march just as stupidly as that drunken bellower whose shouts still echoed in the distance. Who were my real foes? The Danes. Now I had lost all chance to avenge my father. I had dreamed about it for years. When the opportunity had come, fool of a lovesick calf, I had not even seen that it was there. Had my intensity of hate been such that it had paralyzed my will? Rafe had said to me when we had first met in Normandy, "Yes, you are a prisoner instead of a hostage, but you owe your life to the Normans; you

would not have survived three days in a Danish camp."
No, this was no excuse. Love, and that was all the sin there
was to it, had blurred duty when the moment came. I had
looked up the road, but Rafe had put his hand on my
shoulder. He did not have to guess my thoughts. "Riding
alone you could never reach the army. The battle in the
north is over; our turn is coming sooner than we think."
All that day, and the many days of our march, I had seen
not the brambles that snapped back in our faces but a
ford, a handful of shields, not broken, no, but brushed
apart by the hundred swinging axes of the Ravens.

Rafe's voice, ordering us to march, came from leagues
away. I was too cold, too wretched, too exhausted to lift
my pack or take another step through the dank, dripping
grass. I felt Leofric heave my fleece across my shoulders
and buckle the end to my belt. Far off, I thought I heard
a wolf howl; but it was only the big cooking pot that had
tumbled unexpectedly into a pond. Thorkell knelt down
and tried to hook it up, but it was too heavy; his stick
merely stirred the slime till the surface was an opaque
brown. He had to thrust his arm in, shoulder-deep, before
he could tug the cauldron out. I shivered, imagining the
cold, as he stood there cursing and wringing out his sod-
den sleeve. This was a doomed place with its ashes, the
broken ferns, a torn bit of leather from somebody's coat
lying on the neglected earth. We had not feasted on the
eve of battle as the Saxon custom was; there had been no
vaunting, no songs.

Oh, it was wet, much wetter than our Cornish valleys
or the bare moors of my childhood. We left instinctively
a wide space between each man so that the heavy drops

from the bushes did not spatter our companions as they followed. Brambles scratched our leggings, tough as they were, and caught in the mail rings of our coats; we had to go warily, for a branch could have torn a man's hand so that he could not have grasped his weapon for a week. A thick mist crawled into our bones and drenched our cloaks.

The track was endless. It was a question of a foothold here, a bank giving way, a long slithering through mud. The dawn came late, perhaps because we needed light so much. What made things worse was that we were uncertain if we were even walking in the right direction.

"A-oh!" We jumped. Thorkell, with his hunter's eyes, had seen a scrap of frieze behind a bush. He came back towards us, dragging a fisherman by the collar. The man's net had caught in the underbrush and was full of twigs and leaves. It took some minutes to convince him of our friendliness. The poor fellow was terrified, and we could not understand his dialect, but there were sailor phrases common up and down the coast and eventually Leofric managed to make out his story. "He says he was becalmed two weeks ago, just off Pevensea," Leofric translated. The man nodded, and swept his arm round in a great circle. "He waited for morning because of the shoals; and, as the light came, the wind freshened and he saw galley after galley sailing towards him." "Ask him how many," Rafe interrupted. "He doesn't know; he can't count," Leofric answered scornfully, as if a world of learning separated fisherman and sailor. "They were as thick as gulls, he says, when the catch is being cleaned"; and the fellow moved his hands up and down as if he were sawing. "I suppose," Ulric whispered, "he is trying to make us see him scraping fish."

Anyhow, he had raced for the shore, hidden his boat and warned his hamlet, long before the first Normans had landed on the undefended beaches. Now, after almost a fortnight in the woods, he was as hopelessly lost as we were. Had we passed a chalk pit with two farms and a pond? He was looking for a kinsman in a hut near by, who would certainly give him shelter. We shook our heads, able to help him no more than he had helped us. We gave him the last drops of wine from our skin and let him go. He did not trust us and bolted like a scolded hound.

All we could do was to follow our little path (if such it could be called) until we reached a clearing. It must have been another hour before we came to open ground, facing the distant sea. Below us lay a long saucer of marsh. On our left a gap divided us from the opposite hills; it was full of shoulder-high bracken and thorn. There was no life, no sign of smoke, but a run that might have been made by weasels or by dogs led down to the swamp.

We stood in weary frustration upon a veritable peninsula. Ulric looked round helplessly and shrugged his shoulders. I had once disturbed some eels in a shallow pool with an oar; the stream that slithered through the water reeds below brought back my gasp of fear as the black rings had coiled away from the boat. This was a landscape of death, as if all colour had sunk below the surface and there was to be no other spring; even the scar of earth near an uprooted willow tree was the shape of an open grave.

Nobody spoke. We ought to have made the fisherman come as guide, I thought, forgetting that the poor fellow knew as little as we did about this wilderness. The delay was maddening. Suppose Harald was victorious, how they would jeer at us stragglers. It would never be glorious at the feasting every year as it would be for the rest of England. "You were in Wessex," people would say; and we should have to stammer, "Yes, but not at the battle." Why, we should not even feel that we had ploughed our fields. The toil of the march, the courage that it had needed to leave Cornwall, all would be obliterated by our ultimate failure. Then, as I stared down at the grim desolation, it seemed to me that I felt the army. "The King is there," I shouted, "on the left."

"He might just as well be on the right," Ulric grunted, "or even in front of us. There's a road to London somewhere beyond that ridge, and he is as likely as not to base his position on it." His eyes followed the line of the hill towards the sea.

"If we want to reach Harald," I insisted, "we shall have to cut our way through that gap." It was instinct merely, and I could give no reason for it, but I seemed to see the camp while we stood waiting: boys putting out the fires, a smith hurriedly mending an axe haft while the owner swore impatiently beside him. "The King is to the left of the summit," I said again and added, remembering the Leofwen of my childhood, "When in doubt, choose the harder of any two ways."

It was going to be difficult. Looking down at a tangle probably untrodden for a lifetime, I knew that it was full of thorns and, late in the year though it was, snakes. "Wait," Thorkell shielded his eyes with his hand, "by the time we got through those bushes we should have to re-sharpen our axes. No," he looked up questioningly at Rafe, "the stream is shallow; if we scramble straight down and ford it, we ought to reach the top of the hill," he pointed to the right, "in about an hour." It was a much easier way, though it left us without cover should the Normans arrive; but I was certain that he was wrong. "No," I repeated, "the army is on the left."

"How do you know?" Rafe asked.

How could I make the others see what I felt? They never remembered that I had been right before, nor how they had laughed at me for talking about an invasion. Everything had to be so literal, and my mind did not work that way. It caught things out of the air. Only I had to face my doubts as well, and, staring down at the heavy undergrowth, it seemed much easier to decide that this time I was wrong. Yet underneath I knew that I was dodging; it was the right way, our only chance of ever reaching the battlefield. "The Normans landed without fighting," I said, trying to make my argument as logical as possible. "Even if we reach the summit quickly, they may be already there, and then we shall have to come all the way back and start again, perhaps in view of their archers!"

Rafe shook his head. "Stop always trying to take the most difficult way to a destination. Thorkell is right; if we can move up quickly, going carefully of course, we ought to see the smoke on either side from the camp fires. The sooner we start the better."

None of us wanted to begin a downhill fight of slashing neck-high brambles, and so we turned to follow Ulric towards the reeds. At each step the slope got softer and more slippery. All the fire colours, red, tawny, copper, had drifted from the forest to rot underfoot in leafy pools. I remembered, walking with my eyes on the ground, a wild, beautiful tangle that I had seen in Normandy, growing about the ruins of a cottage. The roof had fallen; the weight of creepers and of a spiral of white flowers, whose name I did not know, had forced the walls apart. Here and there a soft grey lichen-patterned stone that was almost silk pushed its way from the leaves. It had been the late summer of my second year, and a group of us were gathering wood. The sudden sight of such unplundered beauty stopped me at the remnants of a fence. I had stared and stared; here, I had thought, was haven, even possible escape. I had reached out a hand to force my way over the stones. *"La Maladère! The Leper's Hut!"* One of my companions, green with terror, was shouting at me from the safe top of a bank. The beauty, the white flowers, turned sinister and horrible in a moment; I shrank back from them in wilder fear than I had ever felt about death. For days afterwards I had examined my hands constantly, looking for white spots.

The sea that had been a line on the horizon was now, as the sun rose, a heavy roll of waves. I suppose that it was thinking of Normandy, but it flashed across my mind that this was Rodwen's day too, or near it, for we had lost count of time. It had been mid-October when he had fallen. Eight years—eight centuries—nothing had been stable since he had left our courtyard on that bitter afternoon. Everything was transient; the greatest exultation we could feel was no more than the splash of water from the heron's wings, which, startled by our footsteps, rose above us.

The men began to chatter; the loneliness, this landscape, got on all our nerves. "Be quiet," Rafe commanded angrily, for we had come almost to the level of the river. "I want to fight the Normans, not draw their army down on us."

As if in answer Sibert screamed, a wild yell that sent

another score of birds chattering over our heads and started us all running towards him. He was only a few paces to the left of the guide, but the grass had given way and he was waist-deep in black ooze and water. It sucked his jerkin down in long, serpentine folds and crept higher as he struggled.

"Back!" Rafe shouted. The whole space in front of us was in motion. It had seemed a flat, green surface; now we saw that it was hollow, a veritable lake of death. Thorkell stretched his spear out for Sibert to clutch, but the man could get no foothold; the tighter he clung, the deeper he went into the slime. Ulric came running towards us, looking terrified; only his lightness and the fact that he carried no arms had saved him from a similar fate. "Get back," Rafe shouted again, for under our combined weight even the grass where we stood began to give way, and the black, slobbery liquid to coil about our leggings.

Thorkell, still grasping the spear, found a small hummock, and with Rafe to help him managed to hold Sibert fast. I shall never forget the fellow's face. In spite of our warnings to keep still, his arm threshed about in an angry, convulsive way, his mouth opened as if he already needed air, his eyes bulged with dread. The rest of us crept cautiously back to firmer ground and scattered to grub up small bushes, reeds, anything that could be bundled together to form a stiff platform for the rescuers' feet.

I slashed away at the rushes, afraid to look lest Rafe himself had started to sink. It was impossible to hurry. Mud flowed into each footstep and held our ankles with the steady, constrictive pressure of a giant snake. I had heard of man-eating bogs but supposed them to belong with dragons to the past; now the comrade whose knife I had borrowed only yesterday was trapped in one, perhaps to death? The overwhelming helplessness that I felt made me clumsy; what chance had we in so merciless a world? How strange Man was, to add to Nature's dangers his own discords! I fought with myself, trying not to think, "but I told you to take the other way." How dared I boast in front of Sibert's misery? What was this instinct that warned me sometimes what I ought to do, not in the bright pictures of a seer, but so obscurely that I was myself bewildered? It was all my fault. I looked guiltily over my shoulder and saw that Thorkell was kneeling now, with Rafe standing behind him. I ought to have made them listen to me. I was to blame; I had been afraid of crossing the gap, and Sibert now was paying for my indecision.

My dagger split the dried-up flower of a rush; its scattering violet seeds reminded me of that holy leaf that was said to bear the man who tasted it to an island of peace, where there were no seasons and no wars. Life was continually June, song, worship; and love merely a rainbow at which the eyes smiled sleepily, without pain. If the deadly dragons of the bog still existed to devour us, perhaps this was true as well; and if I wandered far enough I should find the leaf hanging in a leech's hut, somewhere in an English forest. "Here is forgetfulness," the leech would say, and I should step across the threshold to my ordeal; for once tasted, I should remember Laurel no more nor Rafe nor the little calves trotting between the May bushes to Trewoon.

"Hurry!" Thorkell shouted, and I jumped. An ominous lake had formed about the hummock. We threw our bundles from one to the other until they reached

Rafe. He jammed them down, but they were too few; the first ones sank, and we wasted precious minutes testing our way back to the hill to cut more faggots. "I wish we had stones," I grumbled. But Leofric shook his head. "Too heavy, Master Wulf, they would sink at once; rushes are better, the mud cakes them into logs." He was chopping wildly, and I knew that unless we could get Sibert out before the bog reached his shoulders he was lost.

"Shoot me," Sibert began to moan; "better an arrow than this." I heard Rafe say something about uprooting whole bushes. We scattered all over the slope, like sheep, I thought, as I turned back finally with an enormous swathe of branches on my shoulder. How slow everyone was! "Don't wait," I shouted, "bring everything, hurry!" This time they piled the bundles more carefully into a deep step instead of a wide platform.

"Now!" Thorkell and Rafe together gave a long, deliberate heave as if they were leaning dangerously over the bulwarks to haul out a water-logged sail. The spear broke; Sibert yelled; it was the terrified howl of a trapped wolf, but he was far enough forward to dig his fingers into the reeds. Rafe grabbed him by the shoulders, Thorkell by the belt; they heaved again, struggled, and suddenly he was there, slimy and rolling over like a seal, but able to rise and jump with the others to the slab of grass where we stood.

By the time that we had crept with infinite prudence back to the hill, the rushes we had thrown down had disappeared.

It was bitterly cold. Until Sibert had dried his clothes and we had cleaned the mud from our weapons, it was hopeless to continue our march. We found a sheltered spot under an overhanging bank, and while the others scrambled about to collect dry twigs, Thorkell got out his flints. With all of us at work it was not long before the first flames rose and we could spread our cloaks to dry in the wind, while we sat around the fire and rubbed our axes clean with tufts of grass.

After a while I took a lighted branch and made myself a little fire further up the stream. I wanted to be alone. Hanging my jerkin to dry over two sticks, I might repeat that less than ten miles away, Harald was fighting for the fate of England. Apparently there was a boundary beyond which the senses refused to react. We were warm; we were quiet; nothing else mattered. It was as if the doom and the battle were over, and we were lingering between two worlds. The ravens had not forgotten us; they would come, but fortune had given us this hour if—oh, there was always an if—the door were shut momentarily upon memory and foresight. For once I have a kingdom, the minute seemed to whisper. Now, not yesterday, not tomorrow, visionary and fluid, as if it were a double of myself, it rose above the curling smoke, into the sky.

It was the first time for many days that I had been happy, no, happy was the wrong word, at peace—that again was not what I meant—whole rather, rewarded for a deed I could not describe! A tiny effort more, and I should out-distance the hawks, if I knew the rune. I laughed as I said the words, yet they did not seem incredible; if I knew the rune, I could fly. Wrong perhaps, strange certainly, the Duke and the farm were blotted out and I was absorbed into a new experience.

As if under water I watched Ulric feel a cautious way

along the river, but if I thought of him at all it was to wonder why I should be so detached, whereas the others, Rafe apart, saw only the bogs, heard only the axes? Sibert had been frightened of his death. He still crouched beside the flames, not a hundred yards away, shivering and mumbling. The instant, yes, the suffocation, that any animal would feel and struggle against; but it was transient. What we had to fear—my brain seemed to contract into an extreme clarity—was the eternal round and conflict of the seasons.

On the softest July day among the roses there was a brown leaf to remind us of the long and terrible cold. It was easy to be brave in the sun, hard to think in famine when snow swirled through the notches in the wall. There was always the sudden raid, the meaningless destruction. If we could learn the secret of the seasons, modify their cycle, could not life be continuously my knowledge of this brief second, could we not emerge eventually out of suffering into happiness?

Then we should not be human, one side of my mind argued. Even so, we ought never to lose this desire. How the folk hated knowledge! At another level, priests and clerks hated it even more. They wanted to draw its sting, to have one kind of learning only, and shut it up in a book in a cold room where nobody came near it. Why in two adjoining fields was one crop better than the other; why, if a man held lands already, must he harry those of his neighbours? These were the questions that mattered, not whether obedience was the road to heaven, nor discipline. I had had my lesson in Normandy, the glory of a kingdom. It was less the natural difficulties than the customs and suspicions of men that blocked our answers. A seeker

had to be free. . . . I jumped to my feet again. Harald,
—I must reach him; it was my battle that he was fighting
—whether my comrades were able to move or not.

Thorkell, however, was trampling out the fires as I
came back; my own had died down and it was easy
enough to scatter the embers. We started after Ulric, in
no particular order, towards the head of the valley. It
was bitterly cold, and most of the time we had to wade.
Occasionally a bird rose angrily into the sky. The stream
doubled over on itself in the crazy pattern that a run-
away hoop makes, tumbling downhill. Sometimes we
ventured on a short cut, carefully probing the ground
with sticks, but Sibert refused to leave the river, plodding
along with a couple of companions at the end of our
line. Once Ulric held up his hand, and we saw, far off,
a group of horsemen; but at such a distance it was impossible to tell if they were enemies or Saxons. Perhaps
they saw the bog, for they turned towards the sea. At
last Thorkell found a great stone in a place shallow
enough to cross. We splashed over to the opposite side
and began to climb, not through dense thorn but a little
to the left of my gap, through a tangle of bushes and
saplings.

Utterly lost, we paced slowly along an alley full of
nut trees. My impatience had ebbed; time and movement
were one; all that mattered was to take a step and follow
it with another. The soaked rim of my cloak rubbed
against my neck. *They can't ask more of me*, I kept chanting to myself, though who "they" were—nature, the
Normans, part of my own brain—I was too exhausted
to enquire. *They can't ask more of me*—to break the
monotonous rhythm I reached up and broke off a cluster

of filberts, white and sweet, with that slightly sharp flavour fruit has that needs another week of sun to be fully ripe. I crunched them thankfully till the taste snatched me back to a day when Rodwen had lifted me on to his shoulder and showed me the tiny, black snout of a squirrel peeping from a bough. We should all be like the squirrels, Rodwen had said, storing what we could against the cold, lean days when youth would be over. What good had it been to him, what help to me, to study and save when all we had learned or cherished was looted and lost? *They can't ask more of us.* I wished I were safe and warm in the hollow of a tree, or a hawk watching indifferently from the air, yet all creatures had their natures and their war; the softest dormouse was a tyrant in his realm; birds, though they flew above battle-fields, starved in the winter ice. We ceased to struggle only when we were dead; yet paired with this was our universal longing for shelter and for peace.

The track branched abruptly, and Ulric bent to examine the ground under the bare, black, yoke-shaped branches of an oak. It was slippery with small acorns and the red-flanged, fluttering leaves that had drifted down on the previous night. What an October sunset they were, I thought, turning them over with the tip of my shoe, patches of yellow, almost a water green, sprinkled across the rusty litter of their bed. We were trapped in the wood as all this autumn was, the remains of a summer's life; whether we fell through battle or through age was unimportant. Spring would come, sun would come, but no longer for these leaves nor yet for us.

Ulric held up a warning hand. His ears had caught the slight thump of running men. There was a sound of boughs snapping, and we formed shields, the less well armed to the rear; I felt a momentary anger that this age-old pasture of woodpeckers and badgers was to be desecrated by our axes. I remembered the crash when the first bolt had thundered into the castle courtyard. I know I was shivering, but before we had time to be afraid we heard a shout in Saxon. "Friends," we shouted, "friends;" and in an instant more people than we had seen for a week were around us.

Men came from everywhere; they slipped through the bushes in the frightened way deer scamper at night, and yelled when they saw us. They were not even levies, but came with hunting bows and knives from odd huts along the coast. Rafe picked out the least excited fellow, red-cheeked, middle-aged, a farmer by his clothes, and asked him for news.

"Normans?" the man said, with a glance over his shoulder, "if it's Normans you want, get out of this wood. They're swarming over the country on great horses."

"The brutes," a fellow shouted behind; "they're *riding* against the shield wall; it's massacre."

"It's not war; they're shooting down our men with arrows because they dare not meet them face to face."

Rafe and I looked at each other. It was exactly what we had feared. "Where is the King?" Rafe asked.

The man pointed back over his shoulder. "On the ridge, with the Earls."

"How far are we away?" I queried. "We lost our way in the bog."

The villagers grinned at each other as if to say, we have the key to the swamps, and without us, for all of your fine armour, you'll drown like rats. "It might be three miles," the farmer grunted, settling his steel cap on his head. From the pattern it must have belonged to his great-grandfather and was inches too wide for him. "But the Normans are between you and the King."

"When did the battle start?" Nobody was sure. "At dawn." "No, earlier," a youth at the back shouted; "it was too dark to see the emblems on the banners." "You can't fight in the dark, fool." Each of them had a different answer. I translated the news hurriedly to our Cornish men, and Leofric blurted out with a sailor's frankness, "Do you think the Wall will hold?" It was what we were all wondering and had been afraid to ask.

"It's a good position," the farmer said thoughtfully; "the Normans have to ride uphill."

"If a barbarian is alive tonight it will be to curse the day he landed."

"The Wall will hold, but the best of Kent is dying there; the Midland thanes who promised to help us never arrived."

"There are thousands coming from all over Wessex," a boy interrupted, a child, perhaps my age when I had been taken hostage, who had wriggled his way to the front and was staring at Rafe. "I suppose you think we are running away, but we have no weapons. We treated the raiders as we would a pack of wolves; waited in the bushes till they rode up to us; then you should have heard the noise we made. They must have thought we were a whole army. At the last moment we slipped away through the trees and fired the brush. . . ."

"When the horses reared at the smoke we even got some of them with our arrows."

"Only these hunting shafts won't go through mail." They held up the darts for us to see, pitiful feathered points that could barely kill a bird.

"Well, can you show us the way out of this wood?"
Rafe asked. "We don't want to be mistaken for Normans
and tumbled into one of your traps."

The peasants hesitated. Obviously they wanted to be
rid of us; perhaps they thought we should make them
fight. Then Rafe produced a silver coin, "For mead when
you can find some," and the farmer said grudgingly,
"You can come with us to the marshes, but once there
you must find another guide. We are going back into
the forest."

We turned about for the tenth time that day, and I
joined the boy who had told us about burning the underbrush. "What happened?" I asked. "Did they surprise
your village?" He shook his head. "I was on the shore
looking for seaweed when I saw the galleys. Nobody
dreamed a fleet could sail in October. At first there was
just one ship; then others came; there were more ships
than waves. . . ."

"So you took to the woods?"

"Yes; first we saved the cattle, the women drove them
up the river, but I stayed to watch the landing. They
fired our huts all right; I was at the top of a tree and
saw them burning, but the King will build them up
again, before winter, he promised us."

He will if he wins, I thought grimly. On this raid-free
coast the peasants in their simplicity had no idea of defeat. "They can't fight," a fellow laughed as if he had
guessed my thoughts; "they can only ride. I wish I had
an axe." He whirled a stick against the grass and sliced
off a dead thistle head, making me remember Rollo,
"wait till the arms swing—then strike." Eudo and he had
trained their men for this day, not through a summer
but for seven solid years.

"Nobody can give us back the harvest," a peasant grumbled. "If the King himself sends me a load of barley, it won't be that from my field. I had the best crops this side of the Downs."

"Nor my winter jerkin. We all know what the King's reeves are like; they promise you a coat and it arrives when the frosts are over. Mine was hanging on a nail in the barn. By the time I got the oxen away I forgot it till I saw the fires."

"Were you up the tree all night?" I noticed that the boy's hair was crusted with little burrs.

"No, I pushed farther on into the forest. I heard the old men chattering, and I knew what it would be: herd the cows, watch the swine. The greatest battle in the world might be happening in our neighbour's field, but if they saw me they would send me to pick up acorns. I slipped away as soon as it was light. Do you know our Downs? They are bitter and colourless, without even a tree, just short grass and a bit of thorn. I ran fast there, I can tell you; there are so many vipers though it is late in the year. If we take the sheep up in the summer, we ring bells and beat the ground with sticks. Then, yesterday evening, I found the King's camp. Some soldiers stopped me, but when I shouted I came from the coast and had seen the Normans, they brought me before a thane. What armour! And a great painted shield like a wing."

"One of the King's bodyguard," I explained.

"Maybe! He asked me about the number of galleys and if I knew the hour they landed. I wasn't first with the news, mind you, but some fellows tell such tales! One man had sworn he had seen a dragon dropping Normans from the sky! Of course, lots of swineherds have never seen a sail."

"So close to the sea?"

"Oh, some of them never leave their villages except for St. Martin's Fair. Then they sit beside their baskets and their honey, afraid to answer if you speak to them. They make good baskets though; they last longer than ours; I think they have better reeds."

"And how far is it really to the camp?"

"If we could fly like dragons," and he grinned, "half an hour. Being men, we should have to circle the bogs. If we met no horsemen, two hours."

"You spent the night there?"

"Yes. First they gave me food. Then at nightfall, I shall never forget it, the harpers began. I haven't words to tell you about it. . . ." He stopped shyly. "Go on," I said. Leofwen had told me of songs, so old none remembered when they had been made, and how, before a battle, one singer would start and another answer until the whole army was chanting the story of the race, the staves rising and falling in the rhythm of axe swings. "I wish I had been there."

"They sang of warriors and death and of how in victory we forget loss, all that is past, all that is to come. It is Fate's gift to a man to die while life is sweet to him, never to be old. Oh, it was like the sea against a cliff, for sometimes the men joined in a war cry or the soldiers standing behind me clashed their shields. Then it was quiet, with the stillness I have felt in a boat on a summer day while the single voice of a harper reached up for the stars. I was listening and hoping that it would never stop, though I heard it as sound chiefly, for I could not always understand the words, when a figure came up to us. He wore a dark cloak, but the breeze blew it aside and I saw his armour, grey and wavy, like rings of water.

He was taller than a man, and he said in a deeper, warmer voice than that of the harper, 'So you saw them land?'

"I knelt at his feet, I shall never know such a moment again, and said, 'My lord, they are as thick as wasps around an open pail of mead.' I wished I could have brought him better news.

"He did not say anything for a time, and I stayed there, not daring to lift my eyes. The firelight flickered on his mail, and the singing was unearthly, so beautiful it was hardly to be borne. Then—it must have been minutes later—he asked me my name. 'Oswy,' I said, 'son of Egbert the fisherman.' Think, in the middle of his anxieties and not knowing which of the thanes would reach him, he said to me so gently, 'I hope your father saved his boat; if not, come to me after the battle and I will see that he gets another.' He walked on to the next troop with his friend (they told me afterwards it was his brother), and as they left I heard him murmur, 'these poor people, what do they understand of war; if only we can get the villages built up again before the snows.' "

"Yes," I answered, "the King would say that."

"After he had gone, we lay down because the singing had stopped, and I knew with such a leader we were bound to win. Life would not be worth living in England otherwise. Could a Norman act that way. . . ?" Oswy looked questioningly up at me.

"No," I remembered Eudo prodding the old woman from her chimney seat, "all that matters to a Norman is plunder."

"The fires died down and the men were restless, it was so cold. I looked up at the stars and they were familiar, but I had become another person. Is it very wrong of me? When this battle is over, I can't go back to herding swine.

I have brothers who will help my father with his boat, but I want to serve the King; do you think I could ever be one of his men?"

I looked down at the figure that was so tiny he seemed to be more of a squirrel than a boy. All of them wanted to serve Harald now, Oswy because he was young and needed a hero, the farmers because barns were burning and their Doom had come. Oh, why had they been unwilling to watch a single summer? I must have shown my feelings for Oswy's eyes clouded. "You think I am too small," he pleaded, "but I can outrun anyone on the Downs." "No," I said, for who knew how long we had to live, "if you want a thing enough, there is usually a way."

"The thane sent for me at dawn and ordered me to lead some soldiers through the marsh. He needed an outpost to warn him if reinforcements rode up from the ships. I wanted to stay with the King. They said I was unarmed, but I had my hunting bow and a soldier gave me his spare dagger. It's a good one; I wonder if I shall ever find him again to give it back to him? I took the men across, but I wouldn't wait. I was on my way back to the army when I ran into these men from my own village, a few minutes ago. Now I can be your guide; only," he looked round swiftly to see nobody heard him, "we shall have to be careful. They are afraid of your stealing the cattle."

We had come leagues to fight for Wessex, and all the peasants could see was their own narrow strips of grass. "Why should we want to take their beasts?" I asked in some irritation, sitting down beside Oswy on a log. We were held up again while they chopped down some bushes; apparently even the farmer had lost the path.

Oswy glanced round anxiously once more. "You wouldn't rob us, I know, but last night at the camp . . ." (evidently it hurt his hero worship to speak of it), "they boasted they were eating looted oxen."

I shrugged my shoulders. "Suppose they were; after the battle the King will pay for the meat, and you can't expect a soldier to fight fasting. Do you realize how great our danger is?"

My tone frightened Oswy, and he did not like the "our," for he looked away and made no reply. In spite of his enthusiasm he was a villager at heart, to whom cattle stealing was the deadly sin. Of course it was wrong, but were these ordinary times? The first act of a Norman baron would be to make the villagers serfs. Oh, the overwhelming power of ignorance; it was almost as bad as the brutality of the Duke. Do everything the same way always; make no changes; hunt the stranger. I knew it now by heart. My fingers ached from clutching my knife hilt, I could hardly suppress my irritation, all that we tried to do seemed hopeless. Then I remembered Latif's smiling face and asked, "Is there another harbour west of Pevensea?"

"Yes, fifteen miles farther on," Oswy answered eagerly, happy to be back on his own familiar ground. "It's an anchorage more than a port, in an inlet between the Downs. I sailed there twice with my brothers. They have wonderful shell-fish; we traded baskets for a catch of lobsters. They're good sailors, they go out further than we do," he added admiringly, "but their boats are bigger."

The men began to move forward again, scrambling over a great fallen tree. "They want to be rid of us," Rafe murmured as I caught up with him (Oswy had lagged behind to pick some nuts); "fishermen are always loot-ers."

"Looters! What is there to loot?" A man passed me at that moment in a garment so tattered that it looked as if it were stitched together from leaves. "Oswy says that they are afraid of us stealing their cattle."

"No doubt, but they also want to keep us away from the beach. Once the battle is over their coracles will be out to the ships while the soldiers are asleep. Some fool has told them the Normans wear silk. They will be up the ropes like barnacles, and away before it's light; that is . . . ," and Rafe hesitated because he was very, very anxious, "if we win."

"Gratitude," I muttered, thinking of our long endur-ance.

"I can understand it in a way; we fight over their fields, and soldiers—what is it to them, whose—burn their huts."

"Yes; but, if Harald wins, the villages will be built up again, and if it's the Duke, they will all become serfs."

"Try to make them understand," Rafe shrugged his shoulders helplessly; "remember last summer!" "Oh, the Normans are not really so cruel," our neighbours had said, whenever we had tried to convince them of their danger. "It was an unlikely, isolated instance, your castle; after all, you were captives,"—as if being a captive made one less a man.

The farmer stopped suddenly and took off his cap. We listened. Was it a heavy animal breaking through the bushes, or had we come to the coast, was it the roaring of the sea? The undergrowth ceased, we could see the sky above us, and we emerged, one by one, on to a bleak, wind-swept field.

I can never describe this noise, I thought, as we gathered

132

round Rafe. I was thinking of Estrith. It was crazy to imagine myself home in the kitchen with Egwin's big mouth open, and Estrith trying to make my adventure seem stupid, telling them about a battle that had yet to happen. It could only be because we were all so hungry. I could almost smell the ham frying over the logs on the hearth and see the soft, expectant muzzles of the dogs scooping holes in the fresh rushes.

The din was incredible. It was as if shouting had turned into thunder that had the clang of a smith's hammer, the horrible yell of wolves, and through it all, terrifyingly evil, the hiss of arrows. It was dulled and damped, for we were several miles away, and it was impossible to distinguish battle-cry from moan, axe-blow from sound; only the arrows were unmistakable, sharp and high. "An arrow, a corpse," as Eudo had bellowed from the butts. As the confusion of sounds thumped on our ears, sometimes fainter, sometimes alarmingly near, we looked at each other, knowing that we had to see as well as hear; and I felt myself trembling, remembering the moat and the smells of the siege.

We stopped at a few brambles that gave us an illusion of safety because they hid the view on our left. The bog lay below us, green and smooth, through which the silver loops of the narrow river wriggled to the sea. Far off, the outlines of galleys drawn up on the beach were just visible. It was a deathlike landscape (I was describing it in thought to Estrith), not ugly but somehow doomed.

The next moment all dreams of Cornwall ended for many long hours. Oswy gripped my sleeve; his face was goose-coloured. Half-armed, shouting peasants came scampering down the slopes, and above them, among them, with bannerets flying above their dark armour, the

Normans rode forward, perfectly spaced, as quietly as if they were hunting.

They galloped so swiftly that I had no time to think, no time to estimate their number. I stood frozen until I could see the first fugitive's face. His hair hung over his eyes, his mouth was open, just like Egwin that night the bucket of water tipped over on the wall and he had run in screaming that a goblin had spat at him. "To the marshes," Rafe shouted, and we began to run, the familiar whizz of arrows in our ears.

A hiss ended in a moan; somebody was hit. I ducked and swerved, keeping my shoulders hunched, my head down under my steel cap. I do not think that I had any plan; I was just running, terrified of the impact of the horses. Once we had had a mock battle in the castle yard, and Eudo had charged an impetuous newcomer. I could hear the crack now as the wooden lance had snapped; it had caught the boy just below the buckle of his helmet. He had tumbled sideways over the saddle and head foremost to the ground before anybody could catch him. There was nothing we could do; his neck was broken. At first Rollo had been furious over losing a recruit; it was the only time that I had ever heard him blame Eudo for his brutality. Then he had shrugged his shoulders and muttered that such a fellow would never have made a soldier anyhow. All these memories, these sounds, raced through my head as I tore after Oswy down the hill.

We splashed waist-deep through the river, but I hardly noticed the icy coldness of the water, only cursed the slippery pebbles that checked our speed. Rushes gave under us, sucked our feet down; the clattering of those awful hooves came nearer. An arrow transfixed a water-lily leaf and stuck upright in the root, quivering. "Turn,"

Oswy screamed, and I realized what he was trying to do; once we reached the bog we were safe. A man fell near me with a dart in his back, but I dared not stop. I seemed to feel the nostrils of a charger bellowing at my shoulders, yet in this mixture of slime, grass and tendrils I could only leap, stumble or occasionally crawl forward.

One danger obliterates another. I forgot Sibert, the panic of the morning; all I wanted was to get away from the archers. We swung round in an arc, reached a loop of stream and flung ourselves panting under the shelter of its bank; it was barely a foot high.

"We were lucky to get that good start," Rafe whispered. I lifted my head cautiously and looked back in surprise. To me, the Normans had been only inches behind us. Actually I saw now that we had been nearly out of bowshot, and we were as safely protected by the swamp as if we had been behind a moat. The fugitives from the ridge had been less fortunate; unarmed, they had been as helpless beneath a knight's sword as reeds. The slaughter had been worst at the top; there was a zigzag of bodies down the slope, hardly any along the river. What made the scene so terrible was that it did not seem real. It was a tapestry-battlefield; there was nothing to connect those distorted heaps with life. It had happened so swiftly, was now so still, that even a bundle crawling and stopping, crawling and stopping, towards the shelter of the bushes, failed to waken my senses. They had homes, I said to myself; but it was as if I were stunned, by an overwhelming but impersonal horror.

"Look!" Thorkell, who was lying next to me, grasped my arm. The first three Normans set their horses at the stream, cleared it by a wide margin and, as quickly, foundered. Mud closed over the haunches of the heavily-weighted animals. One rider had been thrown on to his head and stuck grotesquely in the air. Caught by his helmet, he was drowned already. Another was half-buried by his charger. The third, nearer to the water, struggled free as we watched and began to try frantically—just as we had done earlier that day—to rescue his companions.

"Keep your heads down," Rafe ordered sharply; "if they ride away, we can move."

It was true. With characteristic indifference, most of the band swung round and galloped up the slope. Enough were left, however, to keep us flat in our ditch, for a single bowman could have picked us off one by one, had we started to crawl back.

I suppose we lay there two hours. It was past midday, and our clothes dried slowly in the pale sunshine. Whether we had grown accustomed to it or whether it had actually decreased I do not know, but the din seemed fainter. It was strange to say that we slept with the enemy a few hundred yards away, but the morass was our castle. I watched three men, no, four, working their way with brushwood bundles towards the struggling rider; then the numbers began to flicker, my eyes closed and I rolled over into a hollow.

At first I did not dream. It was a profound slumber, the annihilation of memory and sense; then I half woke to find Thorkell lying on my arm and snoring. I moved and must have gone to sleep again, for ages later half my mind said "Wake," while the other half sucked me down into a harassed region where I could neither open my eyes nor move my limbs. It seemed to me that unless I could shake off my lethargy I should suffocate. In a minute, my will said, I must make the effort. Nothing happened; breathing became more difficult; tussling with panic, I heaved and woke to find—no wonder I had had a nightmare—that I was lying face downwards on my cloak.

"Careful," Rafe warned as I sat up, "the Normans are moving." I crawled after him behind a clump of rushes. There the whole countryside was visible, and I noticed two motionless hummocks in the bog. "They shot the horses," Rafe explained; "it was merciful." The third animal had been extricated and they were rubbing it down, but even from this distance I thought that I could see the poor beast trembling. "And the knights?" I asked. "They got the one out; the other was drowned." "It might have been Rollo," I said, and Rafe nodded.

The first years I had often imagined meeting Rollo. I used to see him in my dreams, by night and by day, always in armour. "Ah," I would shout (sometimes Estrith had had to wake me up), "what about the soft-hearted Saxons now," as I cut him down in triumph. I wanted to see him helpless and friendless on the ground as the archers moved over him. As the months had gone by, his image had faded, but not the hatred; a bitter draught like the battle cup of our ancestors, it had helped me to survive the cold, windy hours of our long marches.

I looked up at the hill, partly so peaceful and partly littered with those who had neglected our warnings. Oh, Latif, I wanted to say, for I kept thinking of him too, why did these peasants have to die? They knew nothing about the intrigues on the hunting parties; why did they have to perish on their own fields on an open autumn morning? Or had they, too, wielded power unfairly, turning their sickles against the young weasel and the nesting bird, their tongues against the widow and the stranger? What was the word, the first stroke, that had set these events in motion? I shivered though my clothes had dried, and my head was empty, but Latif seemed to be mocking me. "Solve the small problems first," I imagined him saying, when it was the eternal, the not-to-be-resolved questions that I wanted answered.

"No Norman dead," Rafe grunted, "except the one in the swamp. All we can do is to harry them from the trees and let nature fight for us." He pointed to the ever-widening circles about the hummocks. He was talking, I felt, more to relieve our inaction than because he had any object in view. "At last!" he wriggled forward an inch, "their lordships condescend to move themselves." The horsemen had begun to straggle up the hill, pausing now and again for a man to dismount, turn over a body and snatch a dagger or a coat. We muttered curses, and Rafe had to knock a fellow back into the ditch, who was about to let fly with a feathered arrow. "Wait," he growled; "if they see us they will only ride back again." As it was, they lingered maddeningly, and it was another quarter of an hour before they finally disappeared.

"Now!" Rafe whistled, and from every wrinkle and cranny hardly large enough, I should have said, to shelter a mouse, men stood up and began to work their way back towards the wood. "Not too close," Thorkell reminded us, for we were still in the middle of the bog; but this time we had guides. The peasants showed us where it was comparatively safe to tread, and we kept well to the left of the drowned horses. We half walked, half waded, straddled like herons along the loops of the stream, till we gathered finally at the bottom of the valley, fairly close to the spot where we had started our flight.

Most of the fellows we had met in the woods had survived. They had had nothing to carry, and those at the rear had been able to dodge back to the trees. I had to laugh at the old farmer; he was plastered with mud from head to foot, but, instead of wearing his steel cap, it swung, hanging by its strap over his arm, like a basket. While we had been crouching in the marshes, he had even filled it with edible roots! To our surprise, they did not stop to see if any of the bodies near the river were those of their own people. Before we got to dry land, they vanished by twos and threes. "The London road is cut," the farmer waited to shout to Rafe, "escape while you can." Then he followed his villagers at the slow trot of an ox.

The levies, the men who had come racing down the hill, had lost heavily; more than half their number, the leader said, chiefly before they had begun their flight. These were the first men we had met who had actually been part of the King's army. They had been left as outpost and had fallen upon some stragglers, only to be surprised in their turn by the horsemen moving up from Pevensea. "We should have kept to the woods as the Earl ordered," the man said mournfully. "He warned us to keep under cover whatever happened, but when the first Normans came running by, we thought it was a general rout."

Up to noon there had been no break in the line, but what we feared was that the Duke had a second and fresh army in reserve. It seemed as if our Normans might have been part of it. The Saxons could tell us little, having been at the tip of the left flank, more than a mile from the battlefield. They were confident of victory, though they admitted that the King's men were exhausted by the long march from York; but in the meantime here we were, a group of twenty at most—for some of the unwounded levies had also made for home—standing on a strip of exposed swamp with the enemy in complete possession of the neighbourhood.

The rushes shivered below me. I jumped. A brown water beast, no, it was a hand, gripped the back of my feet. Oswy heaved himself into view, a grin on his muddy face, wet to the shoulders. "Just thought I'd better keep out of the way till the farmer went," he explained. "He might have hunted me back to the pigs."

Our first duty was to re-group. Ulric came running up from the end of the line and I heard Sibert cursing behind me in a low, monotonous undertone that matched the water. "There are three missing," Thorkell said, counting from face to face. Two were easy to find. They lay up the slope, just where we had left the wood, with heavy Norman arrows through their lightly ringed coats. Their end must have been mercifully swift. What was so terrible was that these grotesque bodies with fingers clutching the ground had less kinship with us than the sea-washed crags; the barest rock had more mortality, could be warmer. After weeks when we had been so close together as to be one person rather than ten, we looked down on our comrades almost without remembrance.

I am stone, I said to myself, and then heard Thorkell arguing, it seemed from a great distance, "The archers must have crept along the top of the hill and fired before the charge." We looked up and my momentary paralysis broke. Instead of the battlefield I saw the harbour steps and the man who now lay below me, running up to them, sunlight catching his bare knees, a great bag held over his shoulder as lightly as a cloak. That was a week ago; it seemed a moment and a year together. Oh, what a fruitless ending! He had been lost, cold, wet, and had stepped from the woods not to a welcoming hearth but to death in a battle we had supposed was miles away from us!

The kites began to screech above us in the air. "Bring your dead to the bushes," the captain of the levies ordered; "they shall have burial with my own men at nightfall. A messenger has gone for carts to take the bodies to the church. Hurry, we must get away from here, the Normans are holding the hill." As if to confirm his words we saw some horsemen pass along the skyline riding up from the ships.

We found no trace of our third comrade, then or afterwards. We called him; Oswy ran as far as where the Normans had rubbed down their rescued horse, but there was neither answer nor sign. He must have got into the woods, for nobody had seen him reach the stream; perhaps he had lost himself among the trees or found other soldiers and retreated with them inland.

It was almost sunset. The levies began to cross the river; they were making for a small farm a mile to the north of our camp of the previous night. "It must be that place the fisherman was looking for," Leofric said as we waited our turn to wade again through the icy water. I nodded. How slowly the fellows moved! This corner of a battlefield, the corpses by the bank, would be even grimmer as dusk came, and even if it were towards more danger, I longed to move, to escape. Once it was dark we could neither venture over the morass nor light a fire; we were too near the enemy. At last a Saxon signalled to us. Rafe stepped on to the first boulder and was about to jump to another rock when we heard a thudding of hooves. A single Norman, not a knight but a man-at-arms, rode carelessly down the hill.

"Don't shoot," Rafe ordered, "he may be a fugitive." If he were, it meant our perils were over; and it was only now, as they seemed about to dissolve, that I knew how long and bleak my fears had been! Why, I thought, for five years we have been constantly afraid. It would be like re-discovering the world to look at the sky, to feed the cattle, knowing that the invasion was broken and over. I suppose the man mistook us for his comrades; he came cantering towards us without any precautions. Then he must have caught the glint of the last rays of light upon our axes. Magnificently precise in his ringed hauberk he pulled up, not a hundred paces distant, and shouted in a queer mixture of Norman-English, "Your Standard's down, and your King's slaughtered," wheeled and galloped away.

"In the end," Gwyneth had said, "only the ravens will be happy."

The sky brought honours that we could not give. I had never seen such purple, such scarlet, such crests of fire. If the Standard were on the ground under the iron heels of a shrieking, trampling mob, its spirit had been lifted to the heavens, was spread over us, as long as we had memory, steadfast in our hearts.

We stood up, a target for any passing band whilst the Norman raced up the hill. He turned to shout a final taunt, but even Ulric made no attempt to draw his bow. We were too stunned, too contemptuous somehow of such a messenger, to put an arrow through his back.

It was not only the Duke's victory but the doubt it brought to our faith. Why had victory deserted us? Could the Norman story be true that this battle had been foreordained, known to the priests, that instead of resisting we were merely outlaws? No, my mind seemed to shout; if the farmers had listened and the sailors watched, we should have been saved. Courage alone could not wipe out the apathy of years. Then, as we waited in that cold, great silence with the light almost gone, I thought of Nansvean and Laurel. What messenger would bring her the news?

I pulled Rafe's sleeve. "We have got to move," I said; "there is nothing more we can do here."

"Except die," he answered angrily. "There will be Normans enough."

Then—I do not know to this day how the words came to me, it was a chance rumour that I had heard during the march and had never thought about since—"Exeter," I shouted. "Exeter. Harald's sons are there gathering another army, and we have got to join them. You have no right to waste a man." I tugged Rafe's sleeve again violently. "Half the Duke's forces if not more must be destroyed; and if we unite we can still drive him out of England."

The men drew round me, echoing approval. "The West," I heard Sibert say. "That's our own country, not this beastly swamp." They began to gather up their cloaks and sheathe their weapons. Rafe stood silent for a full minute. "We cannot leave a battleground nor our dead leader," he said slowly, "without disgrace." Perhaps he is right, I thought; who can bear this continuous struggle? Then I remembered Laurel; she seemed to beg me to send Rafe back. Thorkell began arguing beside me, as patiently as if he were speaking to a simple peasant. "Suppose they reach London; what does it matter? It will be sacked, churches may be burned, but we can build them up again in the years to come, make new bridges. With good heart, with troops from the whole of England (for surely the Earls must see that to save the North they will have to call out their men), we can still chase the Normans into the sea. Not brilliantly, not in a single battle to spare the land as the King had hoped, but deliberately, slowly, as we once drove out the Danes." I shuddered when I heard that final word, for we had not driven them out so much as been absorbed by them.

Rafe looked up the now deserted hill across the straggled bodies and shrugged his shoulders. "Take over the command," he snapped. We all knew what was in his mind. Thorkell was at his elbow as he started across the meadow, and all but Sibert and a couple of the levies followed him. "If you think it is wiser for us to die here," Thorkell said resignedly, "of course we shall stay with you." Rafe stopped. I think it was only now that he realized the hopelessness of his action. "Very well," he agreed, but in so low a voice that only those few next to him could have heard it, "we will try to get to Exeter."

Wailing woke me. At first I did not know where I was until, looking up wearily, I saw that several of us were lying in a barn. It was broad day; the sunlight, falling through a hole in the rough planks, caught the muddy toe of somebody's shoe sticking up through the straw. I remembered nothing; then everything rushed in a jumble of pictures through my mind. Harald was dead, we had fought in the marshes, the Saxons were defeated, we had not eaten properly for days.

Leofric's fur cap appeared suddenly through a hole in the floor. You're really just a seal dragging along the ice,

I thought, as I watched him shuffle up the last ladder-rung and over towards me with a bowl of soup that splashed as he walked. "I'm glad you're awake," he said, stooping to avoid a beam; "I hate those screams."

"Her husband?" I asked, and Leofric nodded. "He didn't want to go, she says, kept looking back at the farm as if he knew it was the last he'd see of it. Told her he was going to be guard at the camp, to quieten her, of course. One man from here got away; he saw the fellow killed, and the thane from up the hill and a dozen more of the people hereabouts. He, himself, got an arrow through the chest and another through the arm; I doubt if he lives."

"Was he near the King? What does he know about the battle?"

"Nothing at all. That is, less than we do. They were on the extreme flank, and he doesn't remember a thing from the time the second arrow hit him until nightfall. He thinks the cold brought him round; he heard Norman voices and saw fires. Some Saxons found him, old men coming up with provisions for the army. They put him into their cart and brought him here. He did not even know the King was dead."

The wailing mounted in a penetrating quiver. It had the ugly note an arrow has, on rising into the air. Hungry as I was, I hesitated when Leofric pushed the bowl and some bread towards me. I kept thinking of our two Cornishmen lying in the marshes; they, also, had not wanted to leave home. "Wake up." Leofric looked at me suspiciously. "What's the matter with you; eat, you've been asleep for hours." I did not want him to think me foolish, and dipped a crust almost unconsciously into the soup. Once the warm liquid was in my mouth, I swallowed it as ravenously as my namesake, the wolf. The other men round us stirred and sat up; one after the other they shook themselves free of straw and plunged down the ladder towards the kitchen.

"What are we going to do now?" I asked.

"Do! It's not healthy here; start for the coast as soon as possible."

"And Rafe! Where's Rafe?" For a desperate moment I wondered if he had gone back to the battlefield.

"Don't look so startled! He and Ulric are searching for a guide. We can't afford to get lost again. . . ." And Leofric actually grinned as he rubbed a final crumb round the rim of the bowl.

"Did you know when we went astray yesterday?"

"Master Wulf, all I thought about yesterday was that I haven't marching legs; but you know what I said all the time: the King should have waited till his men had rested and the thanes from the Midlands had joined him; that is, if we couldn't stop them, as we ought to have stopped them, at sea."

"It's all so difficult . . ." I began; then we heard footsteps on the stones below, and Leofric turned a greenish white. I leaped to the slit in the wall and looked out. "It's all right; it's not the Normans, it's Rafe," I said. He was standing in the yard with a group of men. "Time we left." Leofric picked up his bundle and my own (I had not noticed them lying behind my head). "Any noise makes me jump."

I shrank from entering the kitchen, but it was the only way outside. Through the smoke I saw some of our men busy about the cauldron and Thorkell bending over the wounded man lying on a pallet in the corner. His choked breathing sounded worse than the woman's screams. She was sitting on a bench, swaying and moaning, her hair matted over her face, demented, hardly human. As we passed her she looked up with a hatred such as I had never seen. "You left them to die," she howled, "go and avenge them! You are eating the food they grew, while they are lying unburied like beasts." The hoarse voice went up and down while the man in the corner caught his breath in great, shuddering gasps. I felt sick and stopped, but Leofric shoved me out through the door. "There is nothing we can do," he said. "The fit will pass; the man there will die; and we are needed elsewhere."

Half-a-dozen children were trying to catch the hens and ducks and cram them into baskets, but they were too young and too frightened. As a task got difficult, they gave it up and started another, or sat down and whimpered. A drake nipped a small boy spitefully in the leg. His sister, a girl perhaps of twelve, tugged at the harness with her grandfather; an ox and an old ploughing horse were standing by the cart. Rafe had bought the load of food intended for the camp. He had already divided it between ourselves and the other fugitives, and he had found a guide. "Get the men together," he ordered as we came up; "we ought to have been off an hour ago, but I had to find enough supplies. I've advised the levies to make for Lewes; it's the first place where any organized resistance is possible. We are bound for your friend Oswy's harbour with any who like to go with us. There isn't a moment to lose."

All the men but Thorkell had followed us into the courtyard. While Leofric ran in to fetch him, we tried to help the children collect the poultry together. Thorkell joined us in a few moments, smelling of valerian, the wound herb. "The man can't live," he said sorrowfully, "but he's such a fighter, it may take hours. You had better go on without me; I don't like to leave him."

"It's useless, Master Leech," another old man said; he had been dumping cooking pots in the cart and there was a smear of soot across both sleeves. "The fever is in his lung, and he will die before sunset. Go with your comrades; I belong here; my master's slain, and what does it matter whether I die now or in a couple of seasons? Besides, I know paths where no Normans will ever find me. Only could you get my kinswoman away? Her fit will pass and the children need her."

Rafe looked down at the group beside the cart and nodded grimly. "Yes, it's better for them to go. Everything will be looted when the Normans come, and even if they are tired of killing, the babies would die of hunger. Try to get away with your goats as far as you can before nightfall."

Two of the levies had already run into the house. They returned with the woman between them; she had stopped struggling, perhaps from exhaustion or perhaps because she realized that the children had already gone. They lifted her into the cart, put an infant into her arms and sent the biggest boy to the horse's head. She did not seem to notice as she left the gate, but as we turned to follow our new guide we heard a hoarse whisper rising above the clatter of the hooves, "He said he wasn't going to fight; he only had a knife; why did they send him to the battlefield? He said he wasn't going to fight. . . ." We tried to stop our ears, but her voice reached us long after the cart had vanished. "It's no good," Leofric said, pushing me forward, "only her children can help her."

I turned my head just before we went into the forest. The old servant was watching us from the threshold. It was his home; he was the obvious person to leave there, but I think we all felt guilty as we hurried off, leaving him alone with the dying man.

We were on the march again. It was extraordinary how willingly our feet, if not our minds, took the road back! Our feelings had been stretched too far the previous day; they were like wet bow-strings; all we wanted was to get home. Our guide was a wood-cutter; he left the marshes behind us and hurried along the main market road. Speed was more important now than secrecy. Once the Normans had rested their horses they would fan out over the whole countryside, and we had to reach our port before they caught up with us. The man said it was fifteen miles off, in a gap between the Downs.

"Hurry!" The word was passed from one to the other. It was a broad track, and we raced along, often three abreast, ready to jump into the bushes if we heard a suspicious sound. Swineherds often hailed us from a clearing; they had heard of the King's death and wanted more news. Unfortunately our pace was checked by the throngs, often a whole hamlet at a time, flooding towards the centre of the country. Even the smallest children carried baskets; the slightly older boys were bent double under heavy sacks of beans or meal. We pushed through them, but they moved so slowly, at the pace of the old women, we got separated from each other. We could keep no order and scrambled in dripping grass past oxen only to find ourselves at the tail of a new procession before we were free from the first.

Once I jumped on a rim of bank to avoid frightening a little girl dragging a kid after her. She was too tired to be shy. "Carry it," she pleaded, offering me the wisp of dirty rope that was its halter. I had to shake my head. Her father was driving a flock of goats behind her and I dared not wait. "Where is the army? When will they fight the next battle?" I think every group in turn asked the same question, as if they were unable to grasp the finality of our defeat. A woman caught my sleeve. "Have you seen my Beortric? He is about your age, with a little scar near his left ear." I shook my head and hurried on, but I heard her go begging down our line. "He was with thane Alfwine, there was a chip out of his axe by the haft; have you seen my Beortric. . . ?" None of us answered. Oxherds as well as women were in tears; all seemed stunned. A group would cluster around some trifling mishap as if they had forgotten how to mend a strap or adjust a wheel. The confusion and the misery got on my nerves, and I kept thinking about the wounded man. "It seems sad," I said to Leofric, who was panting near my elbow, "to have been picked up from the battlefield and brought home and then not recover." Leofric nodded, and I knew what he was thinking—perhaps it was a race between death and the Normans. Long before sunset they might thunder into the yard and, furious at finding the flocks and people gone, set fire to the farm.

Three great pigs held us up. We had to wait until they crossed the path and a cheerful voice yelled, "So you didn't get drowned after all!" It was one of the fellows who had raced down the hill with us and afterwards disappeared. He was still caked with mud from the point of his hood to his shoes, but he was grinning now and waving the stick he used to prod his beasts. A half-trained dog barked at his heels. His wife and, I judged, his old mother followed him with bundles. We had only time to shout back, for he was in as great a hurry as we were; but it was pleasant in all this dismay to see one family happy.

A hundred yards farther on we got tangled up with a flock of sheep. A grey, bleating turmoil blocked our road, but the guide would not hear of our going round by the trees. "How am I to collect you if you lose yourselves again," he jeered scornfully, as he shoved a passage with his staff, and we scrambled behind him, tumbling over woolly heads that poked between our knees and being shouted at by the shepherds.

We were not the only ones to be obstructed. The animals held up a group of peasants as well, coming from the south-east. One was leading a horse; two others carried a sack suspended on a long pole. We were all mixed up, villagers and soldiers, staves and axes, swearing at each other and the dogs, locked in a mass that could scarcely move in any direction. I heard somebody shout to a young giant with the dirtiest face imaginable, "Hey, Beortric, keep that hound of yours away from my sheep!" I looked at Leofric, he looked at me. Then I caught a glimpse under the grime and hair of a white scar. "Your mother's looking for you!" We took it up in a chant from end to end of our line. The fellow's mouth opened. "Mother's in the village," he stammered slowly, as if he thought that we were making it up. "No, she isn't; she's gone to the battlefield after your booty," the wood-cutter yelled. "But that's dangerous. . . ." Beortric's arms hung stupidly as if he were a clown at a fair. We shouted with laughter and the tension broke; then he hurtled off through the bushes to find her. We could hear the branches cracking as he ran, and Rafe muttered, shaking his head, "Wherever his thane was, Beortric wasn't with the axemen; he wouldn't know a Norman from an ox."

The delay gave Oswy time to rejoin us. I had not noticed him drop out, but as we got clear from the sheep he ran up, panting. "I was talking to the man with the pigs," he explained. "He lived near us, and I wanted him to take a message to my father. This morning he met some soldiers."

"Had they news?"

"Yes. You know there were worse bogs, a bit nearer the sea, under some hills. Last night, a lot of our men pretended to be trying to escape, and the horsemen charged them. They scattered across the moors; of course they knew the ground, but the Normans couldn't see and plunged into the swamps. Perhaps as many as five hundred of them were drowned. . . ." Oswy burst into wild, horrible laughter. He was too young for all that had happened to him in the last twenty-four hours. "That farmer, with the roots in his cap, had trouble with his people. He wanted to get them away at once, but a lot went off to plunder the drowned Normans. The King was avenged, and before midnight, but it is true that his brothers were killed as well. In the centre where the Standard was there isn't a single survivor, and the Duke's banner is floating there. Above their corpses. If only he had ridden with the others into the bog!" Oswy's eyes that had been bright for a moment filled with tears again.

We walked on silently, trying to fit the new facts together. It is because we know so little, I thought, that the battle is unreal, so like a nightmare. Presently an ox cart came towards us, a boy walking near it. He was one of those dull, half-witted creatures bred in remote hamlets, almost an animal himself though he looked too puny to control the stubborn broad-chested bullocks at his side. The wood-cutter spoke to him in his own dialect, but he hung his head, terrified to answer. We saw then, for she cried out to us, that there was an old woman in the cart. In the utter resignation of the very old, she had pulled her hood completely over her head. I shrank back from the agony in her eyes; they were those of a drowning dog. Nobody spoke except our guide who made some remark that I was too far away to hear; but I saw him flatten himself against the bank so that the cart could pass, and Leofric swept off his cap. "What is it?" I whispered as soon as they had passed. "They are going to beg the bodies of a thane and his son from the Duke," Leofric answered, shoving his cap back on his short, rough hair; "she is the grandmother. In the whole village that boy and a couple of babies are the only men left."

It was another dusk when we came to the sea. Was it two days later? I never knew for I had lost count of time. There had been endless marches, some shelter by a woodman's fire, snatches of sleep, long scrambles between blunt, wind-bitten Downs. Thoughts blurred, and I had lived my first Norman winter again with such intensity that a rattling stone could stop me in rigid terror, convinced that Rollo's sword was at my neck. The present was simply a plough, a movement of legs up to the furze, down to the grass. It did not touch me; I felt the motion, but unless it had a place in my memories everything around me was unreal.

How curious it is when days are merely continuous time! Then for no apparent reason a moment rebels, takes form, is architectural; we circle round instead of sweeping through it. Whenever I thought about our flight in the days to come it was this instant that I saw: short grass (there must have been many sheep up here in summer for it was literally shorn bare between the dry, flat leaves covering a few herbs), and a ring of huts beside a colourless sea. "The village," Oswy shouted, with shining eyes, as if, after all, he had never expected it to be there.

I do not know how the others felt. I suppose there was some instinct in us that home was safety. Sibert was now the more fortunate; he simply counted every step he took and felt himself that much nearer his own cottage. Oswy's need of adventure was stronger than any sorrow; his deep desire was to get away from the pigs. Thorkell worried that Penda's men might be loose among the farms. Rafe never spoke except to give an order. Our lives hung on whether we could persuade the fishermen to put to sea so late in October. Yet I wonder if I thought about this once as I followed Rafe down the chalk ruts to the valley? It was more that this hour was so ordinary, so typical of our whole frustrated journey that it became the painted symbol of this part of our chronicle, the survivor of much that was more important, in the distant winters to come. The cold numbed our hands; the earth was indifferent to us; there was no rest except briefly by an evening fire. All is over, our steps said, all is over; only suffering is left and the bitterness after defeat.

We had been lucky. There were still several ships in the bay. Once the news of the sack of Pevensea had reached them, the fishermen had worked all night stripping the winter coverings from their vessels. "You would have thought the Normans would have wanted plunder," the headman told us, shaking his head incredulously, "but they flung torches into the holds and ripped the sails;

there was even some cargo left in one boat and they burned that. They're not human . . . ," he groped for words, "they're . . . they're beasts."

Some men had already sailed, but the headman was waiting for his brother who lived up the valley. He responded to Leofric's knowledge of the Channel rocks more than to the three gold pieces we pressed into his hand. "First I must get my family aboard; then I'll find a place for as many of you as I can. Anyhow," he tapped Oswy on the shoulder, "I'll take the sailor and the boy." He had recognized Oswy at once.

We settled down to the usual waiting and wondering that had been our portion all summer. I counted my companions; we were ten again, our original number, for the Wessex levies had gone off to Lewes, and besides Oswy only two had stayed with us, landless youths without families who wanted to take service under Harald's sons. Only our importance had changed; we had lost the battle, and the sailor and the native ranked higher when it came to rescue than the soldier. We accepted the decision, whatever our personal feelings might be, as a child accepts a punishment for some collective but not personal disobedience.

The waves sucked the shingle down along the half-sand, half-grass circle where I stood guard over a pile of boxes. Several of the others were helping women to carry goods out of the farm. I tried to keep our dangers in front of my mind, but the immediate impressions were too powerful. It was like Michaelmas. The journey was over, ivy on the cottage wall seemed to have burst into crisp, curling flowers. (I saw afterwards it was simply a fallen golden leaf.) A small boy crouched beside a chest, hiding a struggling puppy under his cloak as if he feared that they might not let him carry it on board. Two bare-footed girls splashed into the surge, carrying a great bundle of household linen towards a waiting row-boat. The tucked-up skirt of the nearer girl began to slip, and trying to keep it from sliding into the water she almost dropped her end of the roll. "Hold it up! Hold it up, you fool; don't let it fall! Oh, these girls. . . ." I turned round in the direction of the shrill, angry voice, and saw the headman's wife. "My grandmother's bedcover is in the middle of those sheets; there's real gold and a silk dove in each panel. Traders have offered a fortune for the piece, but I wasn't going to part with my grandmother's work; and now those clumsy idiots think more of an old frieze skirt," she stared vindictively at the two girls who could scarcely find a foothold with the tide coming against them, "than of my cover being tarnished. All they think about is dancing. Well, their dancing's over. . . ." Her eyes glittered viciously. "It's time the Normans came to bring them to their senses." And you to yours, I wanted to reply; Normans would use your cover as a horse rug, but I must not begin to quarrel. "I was born here," the woman went on as if she guessed my thoughts and wanted to force me to be sorry for her. "I'm leaving everything, my herbs, the orchard where my father planted the trees, I can't even take my spinning wheel. . . ." "We all have to suffer now that Harald is dead," I said as calmly as I could, and she turned away angrily, almost knocking the little boy over. "Get somebody to drown that puppy for you," she snapped; "there's no place for mongrels on a ship. And help, hurry, make yourself useful, you're big enough to carry the pots down from the kitchen."

The child shivered, but he did not move. "It will be all right," I whispered, as soon as the headman's wife was out of earshot. Such women were our real enemies, always sure that everything would be all right with the world, by which they meant themselves, provided that there was no laughter, no colour, nothing to break the interminable ritual of spinning and sowing. They had driven the adventurous to the high seas where their weapons were lost to England; they had made the peaceful apathetic. It was terrible to abandon a home, but it was happening up and down Wessex; it had been the sombre background to my Danish-haunted childhood. Perhaps we needed migration and destruction once in so often—my mind sailed off on dangerous channels—to break the clutch of habit, of letting mere possessions be important? Kindness towards each other, the memory of love, these burdens were light enough for even a child to carry. Then I thought of Laurel and hoped passionately that she would not have to tie a few oddments into a bundle and take ship. Oh, why must the innocent suffer with the guilty, what was the answer, why, oh why, had Harald been defeated?

I began day-dreaming about how many of us could go on board? All the Nansvean men had a better right to sail than myself. They had lands and homes, they could not speak the Wessex Saxon. Then my own panic almost suffocated me; I could not bear to wait through a winter of hiding and frustration. There was a pebble at my feet, the dusty grey of the beach with a heart-shaped stain where the spray had moistened it. As long as the heart does not fade, I said to myself, I have a chance. Then I was angry at my foolishness, stooped down, picked it up and threw it into the sea.

I watched Sibert splash forward with a crate of fowls on his shoulder. He glanced shorewards anxiously, heaved them over the side of the coracle, and scrambled in after them. Ulric was already perched forward on another basket, chattering gaily to a man he had met at a fair. Thorkell was lending a hand with the oars. They seemed to move so slowly against the tide, whereas the other boat, the one that was on its way back to us, blew ashore like a leaf.

Somebody shouted. A knot of people appeared on the crest of the opposite Downs. I tried to count them, but they were too far away. There was a cart, a handful of straying goats; then two detached themselves from the group and came striding over the bluff, not by the zigzag path trodden in the chalk, but leaping across gorse and hurrying down the dangerously steep slope. The first one is the messenger, I decided; the other held his arm at a curiously stiff angle; then I saw that he had a falcon on his wrist. "That must be the brother," Rafe said. Then he looked from the newcomers to our still crowded beach, and whistled.

"I will see you get aboard," Oswy announced, just as if he were the son of a thane; but we were less confident. It seemed as if luck and our own legs had brought us down to the harbour simply to stand there and see the others leave. Must they take all those fowls, I wondered; the first big wave would drown them in their coops. Surely a man's life was worth more than a clutter of hens? Then unexpectedly, like everything else on this cruel, frustrated journey, the headman came up, looked us over and tapped Rafe's arm. "Get out while you can," he said, pointing to the row-boat that had just grounded; "we need extra men at the oars, and you know something about ships."

We snatched up loads from the stack beside us and

waded out. The cold water brought back the marshes, and I turned; was that a Norman shout? No, the great cliffs were bare; there was neither smoke nor sign in the valley. Only the little boy lingered, with his dog still in his arms. "Come along," I yelled, and he followed. He was wet to the shoulders before we could haul him and the shivering mongrel into the rocking coracle. The waves were so strong that it took half an hour to cover the short stretch between us and the ship. The headman and his family were following behind us in a second rowboat. "Hurry," Leofric shouted, trying to hold a rope ladder steady, "the sea is rising; you are only just in time." The last view I had of Sussex was a forlorn group of people who had refused to leave their herds, waving to us from the breaker-splashed beach.

"It will pass."
I could have thrown something at Leofric if I had been able to open my eyes. The ship rolled till the seas swept over the deck and out again. I was wet, miserable, and too sea-sick to want anything but death.
"Are you very cold?" Leofric tried to tuck the wet skins round my legs. "I can't find another fleece anywhere; all the women are sick."
I nodded. People died of cold, I remembered; perhaps my sufferings would soon be over.
"It's choppy, I know," Leofric continued in that irritatingly cheerful voice of his, "but we are lucky to get this wind. It is blowing us to Southampton, and at the same time it's stormy enough to keep the Normans in port. They won't risk their galleys in this for the sake of a couple of fishing boats."

"I would rather be dead," I groaned, clutching myself in agony. My middle seemed to be my head, my head a suffering sea-monster that had taken possession of me. "I've been on voyages, but I have never been as ill as this before."

"It's just a roughish wind stirring up the Channel," Leofric said soothingly. "It's not dangerous at all."

The ship plunged, Leofric almost fell on top of me. We swayed and began the long sickening heave up to regain balance. I opened my eyes in the miserable grey light, to see a deck covered with rolling figures and Leofric's rough face, looking idiotically amused. "It's better to have something to be sick on," he said, as my eyes closed and my head fell sideways; "I'll try to get you some soup."

"No," I screamed; how could so loyal a friend turn into such a torturer? "Let me alone, let me alone."

"I'll let you alone till it's safe for you to stand on your legs; then if you won't eat, you can wash the decks down; you won't die rolling about here, but you'll just go on being sick."

The hollow between the grey sky and the grey sea reminded me of an oyster shell; watch-towers and church were dark points on a pearl-like glaze. "We shall anchor in an hour," Rafe said; "did you ever think, a week ago, we should see Southampton again?"

"No." The voyage had been too exhausting to argue that, as I had not died in all the pitching and tossing, I was not surprised; it seemed quite natural.

"It's only the beginning of a new set of difficulties." Rafe crumpled up the limp, unlaced money bag between his fingers. "We have two pieces left, not enough to buy food for a week."

"What are you going to do?" I asked.

"Land first, and see what the news is." He turned away abruptly; while he was in that mood it was useless to talk to him. He would deliberately not hear even if I asked something as simple as the time of day or whether the wind would drop.

Hardly an hour before, we had been rolling in the open, stormy Channel, and though the deck was steady everything else moved up and down in front of my eyes. My legs felt tired from perpetually trying to climb steps that were never there. The women were shaking out clothes and re-wrapping bundles. Lots of small possessions had rolled away and been lost, but now and again a child, searching along the bulwarks, lifted a toy up with a yell of triumph.

Now that we were nearly at the end of another part of our journey, I dreaded leaving the ship. Yesterday I had prayed wildly to be ashore; once it was quiet I forgot my sea-sickness, I longed to lie down in this familiar corner and sleep. We could expect no welcome in Southampton. What were we—a dozen faces in the huge army of wanderers, eating up the city's winter food! The meadows were bare as we glided up the estuary. In September they had been a jewelled mass of eyebright, milkwort and sweet cecily, flat and precise, each leaf enamelled into the other to make a shield's blazon. Now in the dusk and distance the grass itself was rusty, the cattle driven away as if we were raiders (what difference is there between an outlaw and a hungry man!) and smoke rose from fires where fugitives had built a camp. It was less than a month since we had followed Rafe's bright cape up the hills. Boys had followed us, a girl had waved from the last village. When we landed today, would there be a soul to pity our endurance and our rags?

"I shall go to the Earl Magnus," the younger of the two Wessex fellows remarked. He had sat down on the deck near me and began to clean his dagger. The salt had rusted all our weapons.

"You think he is the better soldier?" His companion, I noticed, looked as green and wretched as myself.

"Well, I saw him once; he sailed into Pevensea. I was mending a net when he came ashore with two Irish hounds, magnificent beasts, their noses this long . . . ," he held up his knife hilt, "and speed! Our ponies were a field behind them."

"Are you joining the army to be huntsmen?"

"No, but a man like that knows a good thing when he sees it. They say he got the dogs from a friend of his, an Irish Earl; and he's young. . . ."

"But not like his father. I've heard he has the Godwin sins rather than the Godwin virtues. His brother is the better leader."

"Maybe." The first youth shrugged his shoulders. "If I've got to die soldiering, I'd rather spend my winter where I have something to watch and do. There's a memory to die with, one of those hounds with the feathers above its feet in the wind; you can't see them but you know they're there, and a bit of ditch, not enough to check its speed but enough to leap. That's better than your axe drill and your solemn faces. Oh well," he held up his dagger to the light, "I wish I had some sand."

"We shall get splashed again going ashore," I suggested, "why not wait till we are off the boat."

Sitting there, with his legs sprawled out and a ring of

metal in the old manner on his arm, he was gay, insolent and almost foreign. There were plenty of Bretons up and down the coast. You'll laugh your way to food and a good bed this evening with some girl, I thought enviously, while we, who haven't the trick of it or feel we should hang together, are shivering on the cobblestones. I knew he despised us Cornish as barbarians. I had caught him laughing at me as I lay sick. Yet he was such a powerful, impetuous animal that one forgave him. Perhaps he was the secret of some of the saga stories when a man was helped to fortune by his own enemies? He would loot, laugh, even change sides, and we should admire him; his sober companion, once we separated, would be forgotten in a week. Yes, it's all right while you are young, I grumbled to myself. You can go to Earl Magnus and become his huntsman above men who have served him since their babyhood; you can cross the seas and win, not a farm (you never wanted land), but a collar of gold or a great horse; but what will happen to you if you don't fall in battle but live to be old? Is there anything inside your head except this intense physical vitality? Will some old woman serve and bake for you, or will you be like those wretched tramps that begged for mead at our kitchen door? What will the wagers and the flashing hooves leave you at the end? A seagull cawed in the sky, the mist began to rise, and I think I must have dozed. I seemed to be arguing dreamily with myself that we began with the same amount of coins, but some spent life at the beginning, and some spaced it evenly piece by piece, and that it was just the same at the end . . . when I felt a great clap on my shoulder and jumped. "Wake up!" Leofric was all smiles in front of me. "Can you see the mast there, the tall one, the third from the right? The merchant is waiting for us, as he said he would; that is Master Latif's ship."

A faint light from the horn lantern fell on Latif's brown hand. "I can't offer you much," he had said, pushing us into his little cabin directly we had come aboard, only to have his servants appear with platters of fish and a plump chicken long before we had told him our story. After days and days of hard bread and stew, just to have a loaf baked that morning was a feast in itself and we forgot our disasters and our stiff legs until the last crumb was finished.

"What happened to you?" Rafe asked finally, cleaning his knife and replacing it in its sheath. Dusk had gone, and through the open door I could see the crew huddled forward round a brazier, listening to Leofric and some of the Sussex fellows. "Did you move ashore for the winter?"

"No, I've been on my ship all the time. The first weeks the weather was so unexpectedly fair that I wondered if I ought to sail on to Brittany, but I was suspicious about the Norman fleet. I should have been a rich, easy prize for them. So, fortunately for us all," and he looked from Rafe to Thorkell, from Thorkell to me, "I waited."

"It *was* lucky," Thorkell grunted; "their galleys were all over the seas. Did you know, Wulf, or were you too sea-sick to notice, one of them sighted us the morning after we left Sussex?"

I shook my head. "Sea-sickness has compensations," Latif smiled, "but we'll make a sailor of you yet. What happened?" He turned so courteously to Thorkell that

I pondered, ah, we may be beaten Saxons but we're not barbarians to you any longer.

"Actually it was so far away that only Leofric and a couple of the sailors saw it. The wind was coming up hard, and in our small boat we could keep closer to the shore. I suppose they thought we were not worth the risk of going too close to the shoals. I still don't know how we got everybody on board. Do you know how many we landed? Forty-eight, including the children."

"And the chickens," I sighed.

"Don't sneer at chickens, Wulf; they are worth more than gold pieces here; there isn't a scrap of fresh food for twenty miles."

"They walked over him, clucking," Thorkell explained, "while he was sick." Everybody laughed.

"I went ashore most days," Latif continued, "and talked to the merchants. One of them is sailing with us when we leave, not a pure Saxon I admit, for his mother was a Breton (it's mixed, up and down this coast), but a wise man. We talked and talked. Some people were confident, some seemed not to care, most of us were uneasy. The men were troublesome; they grumbled about the food and the dampness. Waiting with no plans and little work is hard on man or woman. One day at noon I heard the bells . . . then I knew."

Now that the candle had burned to the middle of the lantern, the shaft of light widened. I wondered why everything reminded me of arrows? Latif leaned forward and filled up our horns with ale. "I sat on the poop," he continued, "and thought about my nephew; I told you about him, Wulf, and how the Normans tortured him. What can it be that drives men to such cruelty? Isn't it bad enough to be caught by a gale without having to fear what your fellow creatures will do to you?"

"That's what I always say," I interrupted.

"It's not so simple," Thorkell ventured slowly. "My grandfather told me that they dragged some sailors ashore once from a wreck, and the very men they had rescued plundered three farms."

"So an innocent boy has to suffer for another idiot's lawlessness."

"We know our people; we don't know strangers," Thorkell apologized, "but I feel as you do. The sea is merciless, and the coast people ought to hold together in whatever land they are."

Rafe leaned forward, and as the light fell on him I noticed that he looked much older, or it might have been the white rim across the forehead where the cap had kept him from getting wind-burnt. "What did you hear . . . about the battle?" he asked.

"Plenty of tales, but what was the truth in them once they were sifted? The Heavens were angry; there was a darkness in the sky . . ."

"No," Rafe shook his head, "it was cold but perfectly clear; I heard no thunder."

"According to another report, the Normans flew in on dragons."

"Oswy heard that one, at the camp."

"People were so stunned by the fleet sailing in October, they had to invent fables and wonders."

"The half-Breton merchant came to see me that night and, after we had argued and sifted, our news came to this. King Harald and his brothers were dead, and the Duke ruled over south-east England."

"What else can we add?" Rafe almost moaned.

"We shall probably never know what actually happened. Not a man of the bodyguard survived. All speak of a rain of arrows."

We sat without speaking. It was late. I could see the sailors, huddled in their cloaks, stretched out around their brazier. Latif's captain, he was sitting beside me, had fallen asleep. Thorkell, opposite, was yawning. All they have to fight are winds, not men, I thought, as I looked along the deck; but our minds were sour with our incessant wars, with the blight of Dane and Norman and our own terrible apathy. "And now," Latif almost whispered, "what are your plans?"

"To go to Exeter," Rafe said wearily, "to the King's sons."

"Of course," Latif agreed, "but not now, not during winter."

Rafe looked up in surprise. "But what else can we do?" he asked.

"Come with me to Cornwall." The words were a command. "You can rest, refit and plough your fields. Then, next spring, if fighting begins again, you can choose to whom you will give allegiance."

"Then you think the King's sons will give up the struggle?" Thorkell now was wide awake.

Latif shrugged his shoulders. "I think myself all hope of resistance is ended. The only man who could have united England is dead. If you wish, say it was not the Duke but the northern earls who destroyed you. Your army was at York when it should have been watching the Sussex coast. How shall we ever know now what the losses were at Stamford? However, it is early enough next

April to decide what you ought to do. If you go to Exeter now you are merely a dozen unnecessary mouths eating up the Godwin treasury."

"Good," Thorkell agreed. "At least we can finish the February ploughing. Whether we are soldiers or not, we have to eat." This was a phrase that had spread from one man to the other during our march.

"If the men get back to their farms," Rafe said thoughtfully, "they will never leave them. I am not even sure that I could bear to go myself."

"Yes," Latif filled our horns with what ale there was left, "hundreds will be saying that everywhere. Still, you have no right to throw lives away on some forlorn, ill-organized expedition. There's famine already on the outskirts of Exeter. Wait for spring and see what happens."

"Very well." Rafe seemed surprisingly willing to be convinced. "We'll sail with you gratefully. Only, as you see, we have no passage-money," and he tossed his empty bag on to the table.

"Oh, I shall ship you as crew," Latif said smiling, "and my first order is, get your fleeces and sleep. In harbour or out, from tomorrow onwards, I promise you plenty of work."

There was no wind for two days. Latif sent me ashore with a message on the second afternoon. "It will cure your restless legs," he told me, grinning; though for once in my life I should have preferred to stay on the ship. Perhaps I felt that we had played with destiny enough! However I set off up the quay, past our Sussex boat that was anchored on the opposite side. A dog barked and there was the little boy dodging between coils of rope, with his mongrel at his heels. If a giant gull had dived to the washing tub and snatched off rags to build a nest, the rigging could not have been more colourful. Cloaks and jerkins and aprons flapped about in the wind. Leofric had told me that the headman was spending the winter in his vessel but meant to sail to a Breton port in spring, "and not come back either." His brother and many of the women had gone to a farmer up in the hills till the worst weather was over. I wondered what the old woman was doing, if she was still fussing about her linen, or if she had had to control her tongue now that she was sharing somebody else's kitchen? I could not be sorry for her, whatever happened.

There were so many ships from harbours along the coast that the owners had joined together to hire a guard. This had the double advantage of discouraging looters and of absorbing some of the masterless men-at-arms. I showed my token to their leader and he let me pass; a few steps further and I was in the main street of Southampton. "Up as far as the church, turn to the left and knock at the fifth door on the right." I repeated the instructions to myself in a sort of chant. The road was filthy; it had rained and mud, animal droppings and refuse had caked together in a stinking mulch, out of which uneven cobblestones occasionally appeared. There were fewer people abroad than I expected; lack of room and the increasing scarcity of food had driven the fugitives west. The men had either returned to their homes or gone to Exeter. Only the sick, the helpless and the usual tide of beggars left by any army, were loitering about, hoping for alms or a crust.

I found the door easily. "Look for the bull's-head knocker," Latif had said; and there it was, smaller than

I had imagined but beautifully carved. The man was evidently a silversmith. I rapped and held my token up again, but was left waiting outside until they had inspected me through a slit in the wall.

"Master Latif has sent me for the cup," I explained. Two men stood behind the smith, and they all looked at me suspiciously, to see if I were armed.

"Come in then." The man opened the door just wide enough for me to squeeze through. "A threshold's no place for talk these days, with all that rabble in the town."

Actually, as they barred the entrance behind me, I had more reason than they to feel afraid. There were three of them around me, powerful brutes with great shoulders, and I had Latif's money in my belt. Rabble, I thought; I'm rabble too; we were all fighting for you. But I said nothing and waited.

"Which cup?" the smith asked, his eyes still on my face.

"It was a cup you bought from him two years ago, and he saw you about it last week."

"And then said I asked him too much!" The man laughed unpleasantly. "Two pieces more than I gave him for it and the value has been going up and up! He shouldn't have it for as much again if it hadn't been for these wars. I'd almost sold it to a thane in Gorse Gap, but the fool used his money to go soldiering. You have the coins?" I nodded and he went off into an adjoining room. I caught the glance that he gave his men, and they moved in front of me, ready to spring at my throat if I stirred. What are you doing here, I wondered, looking at their brutal faces; why weren't you out with the housecarles? There would have been work enough for you in the marshes. Remembering them, I shivered.

A key scrunched in a lock; there was the rattle of chains dropping from a chest. The room was unpleasantly hot, full of smoke, and I grew uneasier every minute. The men did not speak; I dared not lift my hand to loosen my cloak. It seemed an hour, though I suppose it was only a few minutes, till the smith returned with a small object wrapped in a linen rag. "Where is the money?" he asked.

"I have to see it first to be sure that it is the right cup," I insisted. He looked me up and down insolently from my scratched leather sleeves to my mud-splashed legs. "Would you know?" he laughed.

"I have learned the marks," I said angrily.

He handed the cup to me and I held it to the light. It was not badly worked but it was ordinary, not as good as many of our Saxon pieces, one of those hundreds with the grape-cluster pattern, brought in annually by foreign ships. It was the type of silver beaker that a thane might bring his wife, when the sons were grown and they had had an exceptionally good harvest, to stand always strangely among wooden bowls and polished leather bottles. They reminded me of the good wife's Sunday dress, stiff and never quite of the family. There was the maker's sign, underneath a tendril, just where I had been told to look for it. "Yes, this is the one," I said and I took out my bag. "Did you say you bought it from Master Latif himself?" I asked curiously, untying the strings.

"Well, actually I got it from a man with him, his nephew I believe. I gave three pieces for it, but a dozen ships were in then; the harvest was good, everybody was buying. These wretched Earls have spoiled the market with their brawls."

So that was why Latif was giving almost twice its value for a beaker that he could find by the hundred in his own land! He wanted nothing that his nephew had touched to be left to Norman fingers. "Which of them was it?" I asked, curious to find out anything I could about the boy.

"Were there two? This was a dark, rather lively sailor, about your age. He had more sense than his uncle, I thought, was willing to adventure more, but he's not with him this voyage?"

"No." Evidently Latif had said nothing about the shipwreck. I counted the five pieces out on the table, took the cup and put it into my bag. The smith called for beer but I shook my head. "Thanks, but the sooner I am back on the ship the better, or they will be sending out to look for me."

He seemed relieved and unbarred the door himself. "Tell your master not to come next year, perhaps not the year after; but in three years' time, Southampton will be safer than it has been for a generation. They say under the Duke we shall be able to ride unarmed from one end of England to the other. But he must change his cargo. It's no use his bringing silver; the Normans want swords, a good blade, a smooth hilt and none of your toys. Or if they buy cups, they like plain ones without carving. The day of your great drinking bowls is over."

There was an air of doom over the town. I tried to reassure myself by saying that it was broad daylight, that the cup was not particularly valuable, and that I had not far to go. All the same, I was thankful when a familiar voice hailed me and I saw Ulric. He had gone straight to his uncle's house on landing and we had not seen him since. "Can't you feel the wind," he said as he came up; "you'll be off tomorrow."

"Sailing with us?" I asked. Ulric shook his head. "No, I've got my work here, and the fairs will go on next year; not all perhaps, but if men want to eat they have got to buy and sell cattle. I was just coming down to the ship to say good-bye." He had on a new suit and whistled cheerfully, absorbed into his town again, sure of himself, divided from us fugitives by the luck that his city was whole. Farmers were moving from the east with their flocks. The day before, his uncle had sent him with two into the hills to buy a place that had been deserted for years. Did I remember the Wessex fellows from the boat? They had hired themselves as guards to a party moving north. He had heard that though the Normans were plundering Kent (it must be dreadful for the poor wretches there), they were still entrenched at Hastings. Our journey seemed to have vanished from his mind, and I suspected that this visit was rather to recommend himself to Latif, a foreign merchant likely to return some year and need a messenger, than to say farewell to us, his former comrades. No wonder that the driven-out peasants clustered helplessly about a smashed wheel-spoke or a broken trace! It was not only utter fatigue after great emotional strain but the knowledge that they were helpless and unwanted. No one remembered the hard, dreary tasks fulfilled year after year. One battle, a few hours in time, reduced the good worker and the bad, the grumbler and the helper, to an absolutely identical level.

"I keep telling people," Ulric chatted on, "there is no reason to be dispirited. It can't be worse than last year, it may even be better." We had left the street and were taking a short cut to the harbour. I was leaping from one cobblestone to the other, when somebody moaned, "alms."

It was an old trick to stop the compassionate traveller and then rob him, but this time there was such a note of hatred in the voice that we both stopped. A man was leaning up against the wall, with a leg stretched stiffly in front of him, in a mass of filthy bandages. Even an animal, I thought, would be cleaner. His face was a smooth, mottled green, whether from wounds or hunger it was impossible to say, but terrifying because it was so inhuman. He sat with his eyes on the ground, but a woman rattled a broken saucer and again shrieked, "alms!"

"What happened to you?" Ulric asked, while I felt in my bag for a coin.

"I was herding swine for my master," he groaned in so uncouth a dialect that even Ulric seemed scarcely to understand him. "Men came, Saxons, from the next shire, not the enemy. They took two pigs, and when I asked them how I would live next winter, they laughed. So I whistled, the whistle I used when there were wolves about, and the swine scattered into the trees. I suppose they were angry, having to run after them. An archer turned and shot me in the leg."

"I heard him cry," the woman said; "he was lying on the ground when I got to him, with the pigs gone and three arrows through him."

"She got out two arrows but the shaft of the third broke; I shall never walk again."

"I couldn't get help till too late; when they cut the head out, the wound had festered."

"And your master?"

"Dead, and the farm burnt. A neighbour carried me down to the church in his cart, but then the wounded came from the east. There were too many of us; I wish I had died."

"Don't leave me," the woman howled, beating the saucer on the wall in time to her sobs. The sound was unendurable.

I flung them the last coins I had; only copper, but Ulric added a silver piece and they blessed us, but what could such help mean? A meal, two meals, a slow paralysis until death was merciful. Then the woman could hire herself out to a farm.

"So much misery," Ulric said, as we walked away; "how can we help everybody?"

Leofric was right. Time was giving me my sea-legs; we had a following sea, and I liked watching the waves. It was literally a miracle, this weather; no ship in living memory had ventured west so late in the year. Yet nature, as if a gift had to be balanced by a deprivation, added to our trials. Sibert lay ill with worse than the usual ague, his teeth chattering and his mind gone, in the shelter of the poop.

I sat beside the iron kettle, boiling water to make him a herb drink, puzzled and a little hurt that Latif had not attempted to talk to me. He greeted me if we passed, but stayed in his little cabin most of the time, arguing with his friend. Thousands of thoughts tumbled over in my head and I wanted Latif to calm them, to say some word that would take the sting from our defeat. Should I stop with the others at Nansvean? Ought I to go to Exeter? Above all, I needed him to resolve the terrible riddle—why had fate destroyed our civilization? To have broken the Danish terror as Harald had broken it, so that never again would a woman wake shivering because she heard footsteps in the yard, only to be slaughtered by a band of worse barbarians—if this could happen, what was the meaning of life? Once I almost knocked at his cabin door; then I drew back, thinking, no, now that we are beaten, he is not interested any longer. We are strangers; he will go back to his proud city; all he has to face are the common dangers of pirates or a moving shoal. If that is how he feels, I am not going to beg for sympathy, to be told as I heard him say to several in Southampton, "I can't ship all of you south." Yet I knew underneath that this reasoning was unfair. When we had spoken before, he had seen clearly enough what would happen; there was something else, and I could not imagine what it might be, to account for his deliberate avoidance of me.

We were due to anchor in a few hours. Thorkell said that the harbour was built on what had once been the palace of old Cornish kings. It had seemed ancient enough in September when we had ridden down from the moors. Flakes of surf curled over the broad, grey waves, and as I sat stirring the herbs, I wondered if it were true that there were, even beyond Ireland, unknown islands? Yes, I thought, Leofric knows more about me than the others; another week of this and I should never want to leave the ship.

"So you have your wish." I started. Latif had crept up so quietly that I had not heard him. "Unless the wind drops, and that's unlikely, we shall be ashore tomorrow morning."

"A bitter home-coming," I said.

"Yes." At least Latif did not attempt to make things seem better than they were. As a child, I could bear reproof, but not the chattering nurse who pretended that I should not have enjoyed what I had wanted. "How ill do you think that companion of yours is?" he continued, bending down to sniff my herbs.

"Sibert? I hardly know. It's two days since he was conscious. He never really got over sinking into that bog, we told you about it."

"It's a slow death," Latif agreed, "but with him, it's less accident than taking him from his patch of soil. Like trees, not all men stand transplanting."

I nodded. Sibert had come with us because his ancestors had obeyed their thanes for generations, but it had been unwillingly, like a beast sold to another farm. He had never understood why we had gone to Hastings. "You think he will die?" I asked.

"No. Not unless those brews of yours kill him." Latif smiled as he handed me a tiny flask full of clear liquid. "This is good stuff for a fever, I have used it myself. It will take time though; it will be weeks before he can walk."

"One of our fellows has a brother, a net-maker, living close to the quay. Rafe thought we could leave him and Sibert there; they can come to us next spring."

Latif began playing with the coloured beads on the little counting frame under his arm. "You'll have to leave two men," he said; "the rest of you will need ponies."

"Why? We can walk home in about five days."

"In summer, easily, but it's too late and too dangerous to cross the moors afoot now. Baldwin's men are for the Normans; and if you escape them, there are both out-laws and ague. No, you must ride, and I cannot manage ponies for you all."

"We owe everything to you," I said, knowing that my voice sounded flat and far away. This is your last chance to speak, my mind was saying, but I could not find the right words. . . . "You always said the Normans would win," I gasped.

"Courage alone, I have told you this before, cannot make up for neglect. You have never seen Byzantium so you cannot know how strange this sounds, but I fear, Wulf, that one day these Normans are going to sweep up to Micklegarth itself. Then our only walls will be the Varangians. Things are going just as badly in my country as in your Winchester; otherwise I should not be tossing about on these cold seas. . . ." Then he continued almost to himself, "I cannot believe all beauty is to go down in ashes."

"As far as Byzantium!" I repeated stupidly. The dying beggar, a flower I had trodden on coming across the moors, Rafe's voice shouting, "time to march," all these I could see and hear; but Latif's home was as remote as what? An olive tree in a church painting? Last summer's happiness?

"Even as far." Latif looked down into the dissolving spray as if he could read his history in its colours. "Follow your destiny, Wulf; you would never forgive me if I made the decision for you. When I sail in April any of you who want to join me are welcome. And now," he was again the brisk merchant, "give your invalid five drops of my medicine at once; that stuff you are brewing couldn't help a kitten."

O NE LATE AFTERNOON, we came back to the moor. It stretched, sombre and brown, towards the horizon of the sea. Our tired ponies struggled over the heather roots that spread a net of spongy twigs across the swamp. I turned to the left at the thicket where the big scarlet berries reminded me (as they had since I was a boy) of the red woollen dots on Estrith's market bag. It was the same path that I had taken in the spring to Trewoon, but another track, not so deep in the forest, led to the forge and thence to the farm.

We had to get home by nightfall or spend another freezing night in the woods. Penda might watch the highway or Nansvean itself, but until the autumn ploughing were over he could scarcely set guards over every woodcutter's trail. I planned to leave the others at the top of the valley and crawl myself into our orchard. "Estrith," I would whisper, for she often fed the ducks at sunset, "what is there for supper?" It would be fun to watch her fat frightened face turn towards the bushes; she had been so irritatingly certain we should never come back from the wars. Her striped petticoats would wobble as she clasped her keys, a sign that she was flustered. "Oh, Master Wulf, how you made me jump! I thought you were a Dane." She lived in a constant but delicious terror of being kidnapped.

It was strange to be leading, and, of all things, leading Rafe. He had hardly spoken for two days. There was no battering sense into that obstinate skull of his; according to his code he had been defeated, and was disgraced by this return. Just what good it did to get killed on an already-lost battlefield nobody could say; but he had clapped a set of opinions on with his first steel cap, and they had grown about his brain like metal rings. I had to smile. He was continually warning me not to be the prey of my imagination, but he was the one who took the old ballads seriously about stamping home as a conqueror or being carried back on a shield. Rather than share the same frontiers as a Norman I would go into exile to the end of my days. Rafe would never get over Hastings, that I knew, but he would settle down and be, on the whole, perfectly happy. He had no lust to go wandering.

A green velvet cape of moss fell over the bank, but the path, though muddy, was drier than in the spring. I kept thinking of Gwyneth and of my foolishness in not having ridden to her earlier. "Some people think, and some people see." Her words echoed in my ears. Rafe thought, I saw, and we could not change each other any more than we could give a hawk's wings to a hound.

A twig snapped. I heard Thorkell curse. We were all nervous. The idea of captivity was unendurable now that we were so near home. I kept feeling that horsemen were ahead of us, although there were no hoofprints on the road.

Bitter the blowing, uncertain the faring,
Will brings the way-lost not lightly to harbour.

I began softly but checked myself. It was no song for this moment, but that wind-twisted elm undergrown with ivy started me whispering the lines. They were from a ballad that I had heard once at a fair up north. One of those wandering, half-trained harpers that Leofwen so disliked had come out of the inn into the market square; it was full of women sitting on painted stools, with baskets of eggs on their laps. It had been a bright, windy day, and I had hung about with a piece of cake in my hand (I suppose I was ten), hoping that he would do one of the dragon songs. Instead he had shouted at us, as if he were herding sheep, such a tale of treachery and feud that every shutter-clap had frightened me for a winter afterwards. It had wrinkled up the soul like a first taste of sloes.

"Are you sure you are right?" Rafe asked. "I couldn't get a gallop out of this horse if the sea were behind us."

I had been certain until he spoke, but now I looked round and began to wonder. We seemed deeper into the forest than I remembered. Not even Rafe could see over the top of the bank, and with our exhausted animals any delay was dangerous. "There ought to be a track on our left," I said doubtfully; but the lane narrowed, and even when we had plodded round the turn it still led on between unbroken hedges.

We were too tired to go back. Sometimes I thought I recognized the outline of a tree, then patches of damp, slippery leaves obliterated even the traces of a pathway. If this were the road, nobody could have passed since my adventure in the spring. Great ferns brushed our knees, drenched our leggings and splashed the saddle bags. There was no wind or we could scarcely have borne the cold.

Bitter the blowing, uncertain the faring,
Will brings the way-lost not lightly to harbour.

I wished I could forget that wretched ballad. "Stop muttering," Rafe said irritably; "I can't hear a word."

"It's a tale I heard as a child about a traveller riding towards some trees at dusk; the words weren't very good, but they made you see the snow spread so that it seemed to melt into the sky, and the awful blackness of the boughs that had no leaves on them, only ravens. . . ."

"I've heard it twenty times," Rafe swerved to avoid a stem of jagged bramble, "but go on."

"I never understood why the rider went into the hut; the song said it would be better to be strangled by the wind in the open than to enter the hut and sit by the fire. . . ."

"It would be pleasant to sit by one now."

"There was an old woman, with grey hair, whom the traveller had never expected to see again."

"A blood feud, I suppose?"

"Yes, they talked and he slept and then his enemies came from behind and he recognized his doom and cried about the feuds to be; but they killed him all the same and threw him out to the ravens."

"Just what may happen to us if we have lost ourselves—have you been here before or not?"

"It looks different," I began, and then I shouted. Ahead of us were two oak saplings that I had noticed in the spring. The path forked a few feet beyond them; one side was already overgrown with coarse grass, but the other was a market track that led down to our village. Some tattered leaves still clung to the boughs and an

182

acorn glistened, it was almost a jewel, in the rut under the bank.

Rafe dismounted. He examined the ground carefully, but there were still no footprints. Nansvean was now less than three miles away, but the perilous moment approached when we had to cross the valley. I caught the harsh, bitter glint of Rafe's eyes as he swung back into the saddle and knew that he was anxious. Suppose there were only ashes and a broken wall where we had left a peaceful hamlet?

The new path was drier, but pebbles, dislodged from the bank, had rolled into the channels at each side. Apparently the ponies knew that stables were near, for they broke into a trot. To cheer myself, I imagined Estrith cutting slices off the special ham that hung in her stone larder, and how good they would taste on a thick trencher of bread. Then the russet pears that grew outside the kitchen wall should just be at their best; they were small but very sweet.

I jumped. The hooves of the pony behind me slid on some dry leaves with the hiss of an arrow. Leofric started guiltily as if it had been his fault. I think the quiet days at the harbour had made the journey worse; how quickly people lose familiarity with danger!

It was so hard to realize that our way of life had been destroyed in a single day. How much less it had been than our poorest dreams, how much richer with its tolerance and plenty, the will to do better, than the Duke's crude rule. The meadows where our sheep grazed had meant harvest and hospitality; now they were simply fields, the price of a coat of mail to our conquerors. Harald was dead. There was no Alfred to rally us. This was a bitter ride home.

"There's a boy in those bushes," Thorkell called suddenly.

We pulled up. Leofric, used to rigging, was first on top of the bank. The grass was bare, but I thought I heard a scuffle in the leaves. "Down the field," Thorkell whispered; "look, the twigs are moving." But I could see nothing but brambles. We stood there, staring first at the pasture and then at each other. "What was he like?" Rafe asked.

Thorkell was not sure. He had seen a face flash, and thought that the boy had on a leather jacket. Anyhow, it was unpleasant. A village child might betray us innocently; the blacksmith's son would warn Penda at once. "Either we must turn for the port, and it's a very long way," Rafe said, "or gallop for Nansvean on the chance of getting there before the alarm is given."

We did not even consider going back. Rafe pulled in front, and my pony followed closer on his horse's hooves than was wise. It was difficult to remember the exact distance to the forge; the path twisted endlessly, with fairly open country on one side and a high bank on the other. I began to feel as sick as on that wretched boat. All the confusion of the marshes came back to me, the figure in the water, the arrow quivering in the stem of that broad, disintegrating leaf. I looked up, expecting the head of one of those great Norman chargers to appear above the hedge. On such a narrow track as this, there was no possible escape.

Nobody spoke. The horses trotted along as if we were riding back from market on an ordinary autumn morning. We must not be taken alive, my mind kept saying, but actually, could we choose? Surprise—a few well-armed men—could knock our resistance to bits; it was simply chance that we were not already prisoners or dead. The doom of battle still hung over us. Somehow, and it was not a reassuring memory, I kept seeing those tiny frogs that had tucked themselves under a useless pancake of weed, in a vain attempt to escape our inquisitive fingers. How far away it seemed, last spring!

Rafe held his hand up warningly. I drew abreast to see the forge, a quarter of a mile away. Up the hill, on our left, there was a thicket. "If that boy ran back to the village," Rafe said, "we have time to get to safety. If not—look to your weapons."

We set the ponies at the little bank. It should have been no effort, but they struggled, scuffing the earth up in little, dusty ridges. I fought an impulse to dismount and run. Here we were, in full view, with a steep meadow to climb, and all of us breathing loud enough to wake dog, sleeper, enemy or friend! No lawful traveller would leave the road so late of an afternoon. At every step I expected to hear shouts or the whistle of a bolt, even to see Penda's men cantering towards us.

Nothing happened. I shut my eyes and repeated slowly the names of the ports that Latif had taught me. I even tried to imagine an outline for each, the river stitched in broad, gold loops on one of Laurel's tapestries, the cone of bare hill rising above a keep. I pretended to be drifting downstream in a light, fast skiff, an oar's length from the rushes. They shone in the dry, clear light of a Normandy summer. Silver was too soft for it; that was alien here where the air never lost its quality of water. I counted fruit trees in my dream, seaweed-coloured nets drying on a beach, one, two, three, four vessels anchored in the green, circular bay.

It was no use. The more I tried to think of pictures,

the sharper was the urge to open my eyes and look back. A bench outside the forge was still empty, but we seemed only a few paces from our starting point. "Don't stare so," Thorkell whispered (he was close behind me), "keep your eyes on the thicket." He was watching the ground as quietly as if we were out fowling, but I knew that expression of his; before a wing could rise his hand would be on the bow.

I noticed that a ring on Rafe's coat of mail was chipped and wondered how this had happened, for it had been unmarked on that side when I had last cleaned it. It must be riveted before it tore the leather—then something hooted in the sky, and I froze with terror. What a stupid ending this is, I thought, all rough edges.

"That may be a signal," Rafe said in a low, sharp voice; "get to the trees if you can." Somehow he kicked his horse into a trot, and I saw his hand go to his sword hilt.

A little smoke rose from the forge; otherwise there was no sign of life in the valley. There had been sheep here, for the grass was nibbled into the matt surface that comes only from much grazing. What did our fate matter to the couch grass and the fescue (one has such odd, inconsequential thoughts in danger); they flattened under our hooves, they were bitten to the ground, but the stalks went on growing. The terror, the joy, the seasons and the sun, that had made Rafe in front of me, Thorkell behind me, could be obliterated by a single arrow, by the same dart that could bury itself harmlessly in the plantains and the daisies.

It was now so steep that we had to zigzag, spread out in line. Was it the hoot of a bird, was Penda waiting in triumphant surprise to strike as we came to the supposed safety of the trees? The Normans were right in one thing—happiness makes man a coward. When I had followed Rafe along the sand dunes, we had been exhilarated, not afraid. What was death, I had thought, a sunset, a song end. I remembered how Rafe had looked at me, as we had crouched under the cliff. "I envy you your confidence," he had said. I had wondered why he had expected me to be anxious. We had escaped; I should never have to feed Rollo's horses again while his men joked about me; either we should board a ship or we should be killed. I had stood up in the wind and watched the rounded, steel-blue breakers smash over the rocks and had said, "Danger makes life *live*, Rafe. I have often looked at the sky and it has not meant much, one way or another; but today, when it may be for the last time, it is full of mystery and adventure. I am halfway to the gods." Only then I had been fifteen; I had never seen Laurel, and I was proud with my first fight, a joy that is never so sweet of taste afterwards.

It was still not death that I feared, but being taken prisoner or having to watch Rafe face Penda almost within sight of home. My knees dug into the saddle so hard that when my pony stumbled I almost went over his ears. My back tingled like a dog at bay. As I recovered I saw that Leofric had dropped behind and that his horse seemed to be lame.

A hoot sounded again, very far off this time, from the other side of the valley. I ought to ride back to Leofric, but like a coward I went on; I couldn't turn. I heard myself panting; each instant was worse, every step took me farther and made it more difficult to swing round. It was as if the moment had petrified so that I was inside time instead of moving with it. I was so frightened that I was almost happy.

It was not Leofric's fault that he was more at home on a spar than on a horse. He needed me. I saw his brown face looking down at mine, when I had lain wet and sea-sick during the storm. At least I could dismount, walk beside him; we could climb the slope together. Duty was a part of life, and who was I to evade it? If I were more sensitive than Rafe to Laurel's voice, if the curve of a hawk were infinity where to Thorkell it was everyday observation, I had less excuse than the others to fail, to run away. Yet my head went lower—as if that could pro-tect me against bolts!—and the grass raced by . . . raced by . . . under my pony's hooves.

"Wulf!" Rafe shouted, "hurry." He disappeared him-self into the underbrush. In a moment the coppice was about me too with its protecting darkness. A few trees really made no difference; we could be surprised here almost as easily as in the meadow. It was only because they could not see us from the forge that we had this illogical sense of safety. I looked back at the round figure still struggling across the open pasture. If Leofric could join us I would never grumble again when he startled the birds with one of his hauling shouts or strapped up the saddles the wrong way.

"You can't help," Rafe said, leaning over to snatch my rein; "and the less noise we make the better."

We waited and watched. How the others felt I do not know, but I was too tired to tug my knife out of my belt. My eyes were open; I had forgotten sleep, only I had been, it seemed, in one position for eternity, and any movement meant pain. Through a slit in the boughs I saw Leofric come nearer, stop, stare at us in a dazed and helpless way; then his beast stumbled on and he was with us, in the circle some wood-cutter had cleared, and Thorkell was examining a hoof.

The trouble was a pebble that was soon dislodged. It lay on Thorkell's palm, a lump of grit with the earth still clinging to it, too small for a child's game, large enough for the fate of man. Yes, like the mistletoe, it could have been the instrument of death. Battle or peace, we walked in mist; and one day no sun would rise, and which of our anxieties should we remember as the cold sleepily, drowsily, engulfed us in its stillness?

There was Nansvean below us.

Smoke curled into the blue, still air. It was dusk; the pigeons were back in their cote. Someone, carelessly I thought, had left the barn door open, and we could see that it was full of logs. The yard looked as empty and peaceful as on any November evening; the dogs naturally were indoors, sheltering from the cold. We dismounted and Rafe started forward, but I pulled his sleeve. "Let me find out first if Laurel is still there." It was the only time throughout our journey that I had admitted his fears might be justified.

"If she isn't . . ." Rafe began, shaking off my hand.

"Rafe, we must be careful. If we fall into Penda's trap, how can we rescue anyone?"

Thorkell stepped forward and took the bridles. "Let Wulf go first," he said; "in that torn jerkin, they will take him for a village boy gathering sticks."

I knew that I must hurry or Rafe's impatience might lead to disaster, but as I ran down that slope I felt as if a dozen Normans were watching me. I expected an arrow to whistle through the air or a horseman to gallop out. A bit of courage returned when I was not hailed, but I felt much better when I was hidden again in the ditch at the bottom of the orchard. Nansvean looked peaceful enough, but I had not liked the barn door being open; it was unlike Estrith if she still had charge of the kitchen. Still, nobody had discovered my loose sticks in the palisade. The outer bark was almost peeled away, but I soon found the scratch I had made, so that I knew which stick to pull. The ground was hard and it took me a moment to force them apart, and after I had wriggled through I was up to my knees in long, dripping grass. I kicked my way between the coarse tufts until I got to the path that led to the pond.

The white ducks were quacking at the muddy edge. The apple trees were bare. It was like any autumn evening when we finished our tasks hurriedly so as to get back to the warmth of the big fireplace. A duck waddled up, and somehow just the way that it opened its beak as if to question me made me realize again how the old, easy, tolerant life had gone; we were the hunted now in our own land. My hands tingled and my face burned; I felt struck not by lightning but by rage. Then I saw Laurel standing beside a bush with an almost empty basket at her feet. I gave my hunting bark, and she jumped.

"Is it safe?" I whispered. "Is Penda here?"

"Wulf," she said, "oh, Wulf," and kissed me.

"Rafe is here, in the wood," I still spoke softly, "is it safe?"

The five little stones that I had tumbled into the pond that July day still shone there, but Laurel had changed. "It's as safe here," she murmured distastefully, "as anywhere in England." Then I knew that she had heard about Harald. She went on emptying the last grains from the basket, and the greedy old duck we called the Pirate pecked at the fringes of her apron. "I hoped, but I did not know. . . ." she said, and looking at her face I saw how it had altered. How we all had altered; for it was less a summer that had gone than an utter transformation, so that we even moved in a slower, different way. Leofwen's song of the nine maidens came into my mind, the heedless, careless circle, the sudden freezing into stone. Even the colour seemed to have gone from Laurel's hair as she turned away from the pond. "I always knew, Wulf, that you would come back."

"Leofwen said," I reminded her, "that I wasn't born to be brought home on my shield." At that word Laurel seemed to come alive. "Where is he, where have you left him, is he hurt?"

"Not to matter. Only his pride. He is sulking because he feels he has been defeated."

"Men are so stupid," Laurel said, following me up the hill, "unless they are philosophers, Wulf, as you are."

We did not go back through the palisade, but kept to the ordinary path. We waved and shouted, and Rafe came running to meet us, leaving Thorkell and Leofric to follow with the ponies. Familiar as it was, nothing seemed real; perhaps I had dreamed of it too much? "This is a moment that should last forever," Laurel whispered. "I was afraid . . . so afraid."

Rafe slowed into a walk when he was within a few paces of us. "Here I am," he grumbled, "shipwrecked for the second time, without honour and without horsemen." Still, he seemed pleased to find Laurel in his arms.

We let them wander off alone and led the ponies to the yard. How bleak the stones looked under the winter sky; it was grey, it was dark, apart from a faint glow to westward. Once we had found a worn, gold cup under some roots in the moor. I had watched, standing a little behind Leofwen, while two herdsmen had grubbed it out and held it up to the light; then they had scoured it in the stream until a scratched pattern showed clear under the water. It had come from a king's court, we had argued; but Rodwen had shaken his head and muttered, "Roman." Who was its owner, had he been killed, had he gone south to escape the raiders and never been able to return? "They buried their plunder, just as we do before the Danes." I could hear the voices above me as I had sat cross-legged that evening beside the fire. "No, there were neither bones nor spear heads; it was no battle; somebody buried it hastily and never was able to find the place again." The men had turned the bowl round in their fingers, each inventing another story; and I had looked at the painted sticks that were my playthings and felt for the first time how mortal, how transient all life was. Not that I had put it into such words—I was perhaps eight. I had simply shivered in the fire-light and wondered of what use it was to love even my dog, when a moment could separate us from each other? Death and loss, they were already nearer to me than I knew. None of us had wanted to keep the cup, there was a terrifying sadness about it; and eventually the finder had taken it to the church at York. Only as I looked up now at the setting sun, it was just that same faint gold that had shone through the scales of crusted, powdery earth.

It did not take us long, working together, to stable the

horses and hurry to the kitchen. Gradually over supper we pieced our news together. The village had known of the battle in an incredibly short time. The tale had passed from hamlet to hamlet across England as swiftly as a horse could run or a hawk fly. In some places church bells had summoned a parish to mourn, but in others the clergy had been openly joyful over the Duke as conqueror. "How did you actually hear?" I asked, swallowing the last morsel of a huge slice from Estrith's finest ham; "we were afraid that we should find you expecting us as victors."

"I think I knew when you left." Already something of the old life and warmth had come back into Laurel's voice. "The first week was worse than any of the others, but I never got used to your leaving, Rafe; this very afternoon was just as hard to bear as the day you galloped out of the valley. I felt I could not go on living; then Estrith bullied me. I don't know if I should have survived if it had not been for Estrith." She leaned forward and patted the cook's plump arm. "She made me work so hard that I had no time to think."

"There was too much to do," Estrith grumbled indignantly, looking as reproachfully at Thorkell as if he had simply gone to St. Martin's fair. "With all you men away I had the kitchen garden to dig myself, as well as looking after the hams and drying the herbs."

"We went out for the blackberries," Laurel continued, "but as I pulled the branches down I wondered why we toiled so hard only to begin afresh every autumn? There's a lot of prayers in the syrup, Rafe; each time I picked a berry, I prayed for your safety."

"It's going to be a hard winter," Estrith broke in, shaking her head gloomily, "the birds left early." Thorkell nodded, nibbling at his ham bone with the intentness of a dog.

"October came and with it a feeling of doom in the air that we all noticed. You couldn't walk along the village street without somebody talking to you about the comet. Nothing went right, and if I tried to spin, Rafe, I thought about you till my threads ravelled. The dogs missed Wulf; they raced out every morning to look for him and trailed back, whimpering. Then came one of those bright, clear mornings that snare you into thinking winter will be late when it is really just round the corner. I had a crazy idea that I might see your ship, and Estrith wanted some cockles. So we went off to the shore, and there was still a bit of thyme in flower by that rock where we always sat; and it made me happy. I felt it was a good omen; then I thought I was foolish. . . ."

"Not so foolish," Rafe teased.

"We found some dry boulders, and the sea was so blue it might have been June, when suddenly I had an impulse to go home. 'Suppose a messenger should come,' I said, 'and nobody knows where we are; he might ride away.'"

"With me, it wasn't a silly notion," Estrith protested; "it was rheumatism. You can say what you like, Leofric, about salt water; I know it makes my knees tingle when I go to bed."

"So we walked back, and I noticed that by the time we got to the lane we were almost running. There was a queer silence about the day as if we were going to have a thunderstorm; only then it got cold. It was the fourteenth of October. We lit a fire, but all evening I was shivering. . . ."

"She caught a touch of ague in the marshes," Estrith explained.

"I was afraid to sleep. The wind turned into shouts, the shadows into the dying; there was the terrible rhythm of the rising axes. Then a man seemed to set his horse at a wall; I could see his lifted sword. . . ."

"She had a nasty touch of fever," Estrith snorted; "every time the shutters rattled she thought it was arrows."

"I saw men crumple like that stag that fell into the gully; I looked for you and was afraid to see you, yet I felt you were there."

"We should never have gone sitting on those rocks in the first place; and then Mistress Laurel would come back by way of the swamp. She said it took less time."

"Anyhow it was four days before I felt like spinning again, or was it longer? I only got up because I was ashamed to lie in bed with Estrith working so hard. My mind felt easier; what was to happen had happened, and now there was nothing to be done about it, one way or the other. Then, the first afternoon I came downstairs, we went to the barn to tie up herbs and Egwin called us. He had been chopping down an old tree, and his axe had broken. He wanted to borrow ours. I was standing on the ladder (I shall always remember it), and as he came into the yard he shouted, 'They say King Harald is dead.' 'Dead?' 'Shot through the helmet with an arrow.'

"I asked Egwin if we had been defeated, but he scratched his ear and said he didn't know."

"They won't understand even now," I interrupted hotly. "The people blame Harald, but they would not follow him; they laid up the ships. Our only chance was to intercept the fleet. At sea, they couldn't have used the new tactics. There is blood guilt on them. . . ." Then I stopped, for I saw Rafe looking at me sorrowfully.

"Ah, Wulf," Laurel said in the calm, soft voice that throughout our journey I had so longed to hear, "village people see the seasons rather than the kings; they will learn soon enough when they can fish their own rivers no longer, and a new master piles their harvest in his barn."

The torches were burning down, the fire dying away. As I looked up at Laurel in the darkness I seemed to see the figure of Latif's compassionate little goddess. Both had the same tranquillity, the same glow—was it ivory or flesh?—something not motionless at all but full of something beyond us, like the runes on the great swords. Mercy, I thought, yes, it is right to be merciful, but have we not also to ask ourselves: where does mercy end? The English had refused to listen, refused to arm; they had been unwilling to defend a way of life centuries ahead of William's brutal plundering, until it had been too late. The Normans had had friends everywhere, weaving a net from east to west; and we had not only let them snare us, we had helped them! What of the web of evasion and appeasement we had spun about our liberties? Only Harald had fought, and, whatever the Godwin sins might be, I was his thane always. To understand too well, to forgive too often, was this a way to peace?

"It was not your fault, Wulf." Laurel put her hand upon my shoulder. "You did everything you could to warn us."

I dared not spoil her joy at our return. Leofric was already snoring, with his head on the table. Thorkell's

196

mouth was open, his eyes were closed, he leaned back against the wall with his long legs thrust out in front of him. "Time to sleep," Rafe said, getting up and stretching himself; "tonight we should be safe, even from dreams." He smiled at me; he wanted to be kind. "We should never have got back without you, Wulf. You know, Laurel, if he had not kept after me like a dog at one's heels, I should be lying now at Hastings." Then Laurel kissed me again and whispered—but all she thought about was Rafe—"Whatever happened, you were not defeated."

I opened the door to let out the smoke and to look once more at the sky. It was as cold, as still—another tale came into my head—as if this were the threshold of the twins, sleep and death. I heard far off the hooves of Norman chargers; tonight they thudded only in my imagination; but in a week, or a month, or a year they would gallop into the yard and summon us. This was a threatened sanctuary. Rafe closed gently the door of Laurel's room. The men and the dogs lay on the rushes around the fire. Our adventure was over. Neither Laurel nor the land wanted me. Everything I desired had been taken from me in a single day.

It was late next morning before I woke up. After all, I had had no nightmares. I hated crawling from under my fleeces, but Estrith had left, thoughtfully, my old winter jerkin hanging on a stool. I pulled it on and went slowly downstairs. The wind was howling down the valley; we had come home just in time. I thought I heard the gulls, and there was the familiar, constant burr of the stream below the elms. The kitchen was empty, but as I opened the door I heard voices in the courtyard. "You see, Rafe," Laurel was saying, "there is really no need to be afraid."

"But how do you know that Penda is dead?" Rafe had an irritating way of sounding incredulous about the most matter-of-fact statements. I jumped. The previous evening we had purposely avoided mentioning him, but Penda had been constantly in our thoughts.

"It was Egwin again who brought me the news." Laurel was standing at the end of the yard in the cloak that I liked so much; the weave reminded me of the fanlike, fragile sea moss. "Afterwards the Abbot told me. Penda was riding to Bodmin to join Count Baldwin."

"After loot," Rafe snorted grimly.

"We think," Laurel continued, "that he was going to ask him for my estates."

There was a pause. It was what we had feared ever since Hastings. We were as helpless as hares, to add to our other troubles. In the eyes of the Duke we were all outlaws; and whether Laurel had been married a year or a day, the land was his, by right of battle. Even if Rafe were willing to submit himself, what chance of pardon had a man who had been with Harald?

"Sometimes Fate is merciful, Rafe. There was a fight on the moors, and one of the outlaws slew Penda."

I saw it! I saw it! The grey mist, a cairn of stones, heather rolling for miles, ancient earth, Thor's land, that Penda had violated. Had he triumphed we should not even have had the rough justice of the Norman soldier. A knight, at least, would have wanted to draw arms and horses from his farm, but such a brawler would have let the ditches fill, the brambles grow, for all he would have cared about them. The fields would have gone back to moor, to no man's pasture. Docks would have sprung where barley rotted. Then (the gods had so willed it), men had ridden out of the mist with axes and arrows. Free folk whom Penda himself had driven into exile and misery. A horse had screamed as a bolt had hit it; men had sprung from the moor and blended back into the moor, no better than the beasts that he had flung them out to join. The feasting, the boasts and the ride to Bodmin had finished with the ravens as master. It was a seemly end.

"I shall believe that the fellow is dead when I see his corpse," Rafe muttered eventually. "How do we know that it is not just a tale?"

"No, Rafe," Laurel said firmly, "some charcoal-burners found the bodies. The horses and the weapons had been taken, but the Abbot saw . . . the head. No man now will ride across that moor."

"He left no heir?"

"The nephew was killed with him, so the lands will go to the Count."

"And ours? What mercy is there," I heard the bitterness in Rafe's voice, "for us who followed Harald?" I knew what he was thinking; the outlaws and ourselves, though our motives were so different, were branded with the same token. In the eyes of our Norman masters we were dispossessed and serfs.

"I have spoken to the Abbot."

"Oh, Laurel, was that wise?"

"Yes, Rafe," Laurel hesitated for a moment, "I have given the Priory those two farms beside the Goon."

I could see Rafe's hand go to his sword, but Laurel was smiling at him and she put her fingers over the hilt. "Listen, dear, it could have been much worse. The Abbot is a good farmer, and he knows another when he sees one. We had to pay some fine for . . . our mistakes. The Abbot said if you came back, and I didn't know then if I should ever see you again, it must seem as if you had turned round at the port. Only I have promised, Rafe, and you must help me, that we will go to the Abbot's church."

Rage was choking me or I would have shouted, no, Rafe, you can't do that; you can't surrender to the enemy, for then the Abbot would have his way, this corner would be no longer Cornish, in another generation it would be Norman. I saw Gwyneth holding the heather against her cloak. "Royal purple," she had said, smiling, "to match the bells on King Arthur's horse." Why should this alien race extinguish us, blot out Alfred's glory, destroy not Godwin's gold but our true treasure, memory, so that the children on the green, the harpers in the yard, would laugh in a few years at our "barbarian darkness"?

Rafe stood with his eyes fixed on the flat courtyard stones. His hand still played with his sword. He did not speak. "Rafe dear," Laurel went on, "try to think of me. Where will your fighting end? In your being stabbed like Penda on some moor. Then I shall have to cede Nansvean to the first Norman who covets it, and count myself lucky if I have a hovel to sleep in, without husband or bread. The Abbot likes us; we shall be protected. You can till your land any way you will, and for that what have you to promise? Merely to conform for an hour or two, on holy days."

They were silent for a long time. What Laurel said was reasonable, yet there was something—and I felt my heart beating—beyond reason. There was Latif's voice, "Soon it will be spring; remember me." If parting had to come, it was better that I knew now, before I had had time to settle down . . . or hope.

Rafe was playing with the tassels on Laurel's cloak; a line of silver flashed in the bright morning air. "Wulf will never submit," I heard him say, and was extravagantly glad.

"Time may quiet even him," her voice was less confident, "what can he do against an army?" Then she took Rafe by the arm and led him out of the gate; they began to chatter about the trees as if nothing had happened. They stood for a moment by the wall where there were still a few red berries hanging on a bush. I thought that they were going to fetch a ladder and look over the apples in the barn, but instead they turned towards the village. It was the path that led to the church.

I hope that I never have to live through another such winter. It was imagination, perhaps, but it seemed unnaturally cold, as if nature were mourning Harald's death. I shivered under the heaviest sheepskins. The stream was swollen with black, angry looking water and the winds blew till the very cliffs rocked. It was strange. Rafe said that time flew. To me, every day was a year, every minute an hour. Work lost its purpose, and I wandered helplessly in that grey land where no light is, a land of outlaws who die, they say, unforgiven and unavenged.

I hungered for news and could hardly bear to listen to it when it came. For days we heard nothing of the Duke. It was so wild that village was cut off from village; the snow defended us where swords had failed. When at last word came (it was at our Christmas feast) that London was plundered, the Godwin lands ravaged, people spoke of the Normans as if they were merely raiding Scots. "Harald," an old man said, sitting close to the fire with a part of a bridle in his hand, "what was he after but gold? You young folks," he shook the reins at us, "riding to Wessex, riding back again with the harvest spoiling on the fields, all you wanted was change." He began to polish the bit with a scrap of leather the colour of his cheeks, simply because his fingers had to move. "Kings die, Earls fall, but our real ruler is winter," he chuckled to himself and rubbed the leather up and down; "and how do you fight winter? With sheep and barley, not with axes and boasts." Everybody laughed and his neighbour passed him a horn full of ale.

They would not see, could not know. I held my tongue; Laurel was watching me. Sometimes she smiled at me in the old way, but at table she stopped the talk at once if it went back to Hastings. I often woke in the middle of the night to wonder if it were just prudence, her love for Rafe, a deliberate attempt to still the village passions before Count Baldwin rode over in the spring, or if she had accepted the Conqueror loyally? I would frame brave speeches as the night slipped by: I do not blame you, Laurel, if you really believe you can save your friends by joining the Abbot's party, but are you sure you are right? Priests and kings cannot help us; each of us, ultimately, has to struggle alone for salvation. Surely resistance is important just because we are powerless? What will you do when you have to send your own sons to Baldwin's castle to be trained in the Norman way? Neither the Abbot's influence nor your own gentleness can keep them at home, and they will come back strangers. The words would spin themselves in the darkness, but when day came, if I passed through the hall where Laurel sat at her wheel, we smiled and said nothing, fearing to hurt each other.

Rafe had invited everyone for the customary supper, though we were short of food even at the farm. The age of plenty had gone; the rains had rotted what should have hung in the larder, the crops had been poor. In living memory, nobody had seen so many rats; we had spent hours about the draughty barns, chasing and killing them, only to find that they had quadrupled the next week. The folk grumbled, but not at our conquerors; they found fault rather with us, as if we could help the weather, the taxes or the decay that rotted the sacks with mould and turned the cider sour.

Some distrusted the Normans and feared the coming spring; the rest were ready to accept their new masters. They wanted change even if it brought them chains! The previous year I had heard under the coarse words of our rough country songs, the echo of a triumphant past. Tonight they seemed flat and ugly; no effort of will could transpose these jingles into Camelot's songs. I should have gone to the barn and stayed with my own thoughts, but I had to carve joints and pass the dishes. Then Egwin's bellow reached my ears. "Harald," he proclaimed, "how could Harald rule England? He always had a wine cup in his hand."

I had never known Egwin let a horn of beer pass him by, but I stopped carving to listen.

"And women! They took our tithes and called it ship money, but how was it spent? Ask the foreigners, the linen merchants. I wouldn't allow my daughter to wear one of those kirtles; you can see right through them."

"Yes," Estrith stooped over the board and tried to

scratch away a blob of tallow, "they say the Duke has never looked at a woman except his wife. There's an example for you! Our young folk need discipline. They are always wanting this, wanting that, even to choose their own husbands. . . ."

"And leave them," Egwin finished with a gale of laughter.

"And now, except for the old mother and her brood at Exeter, all the Godwins are dead or prisoners. It's a sad thing when a great family is cut off like an old tree and its fruit is barren."

"They brought it on themselves," one after the other the heads round the table nodded.

"Yes, they were proud, sometimes too proud to go to church, and look where it has led them?"

"We were a godless land and let any deny it who can." Egwin held out his horn to be refilled. "And now we are judged for the Godwin sins." He emptied the freshly poured beer at a gulp.

"How could any leader save a land that split like rotten wood?" I was surprised myself at the fury in my voice. "All he had was his own army, and the flower of it died at Stamford. It was nothing, was it, the march of York, the fighting, the return to Sussex? Have you no memory, no gratitude? If it had not been for the new weapons, and Harald warned you about them, he would still be King."

They looked at me in silence, with hatred in their eyes. "Surely the Danish raids taught us to be united? William's army is a single lance at his command. If his knights question him, there is no riding away to their castles; he kills them. That was Harald's fault if you like; he forgave, he was too kindhearted, it was his own Saxons who betrayed him. . . ." I thought of the thanes and farmers who had sat drinking in their halls while the Normans landed on our sands.

I was shouting, I suppose, but such groups all over England had cost us our freedom. I knew their talk. They didn't want to stand up for themselves; they wanted a ruler, to bargain with him and grumble. I stood up; in another moment I might have knocked Egwin down, but Laurel thrust a torch into my hand. "I wish you would light me down to the cellar, Wulf; we need more ale."

As soon as we moved they started chattering again; the faces grew in the flickering torchlight into mummers' masks, straw giants, the group a boy imagines in the night when he dreams of a doomed feast and the blood feuds following it. A pointed hood nodded backwards and forwards, throwing the shadow of a gigantic beak on the wall. Our Christmas merriment was sour; they were jeering now at some stupid girl who had stayed a moment too long with the shepherds. Laurel unlocked the door at the bottom of the steps, but it was only when we were in the cellar that she spoke. "For Rafe's sake, Wulf, it is better to be silent. Men like Egwin will never understand."

"I will not have Harald misjudged."

"We shall all remember Harald to the end of our days, but we need peace too. The times have been so troubled. Why, you said yourself last spring, you wondered if it was worth while sowing the fields. If the Duke is strong, if he clears the roads. . . ." I could see that she was thinking of Penda. "Can't you make the best of what we cannot change?"

"Harald would have done the same if he had lived."

I did not want to hurt Laurel, but we had to be just.

The lawlessness had come from the Normans; for twenty years they had sapped our traditions and set us against each other. She watched in silence while I filled one of the jugs; then she whispered, as if even here she feared to be overheard, "Promise me you won't go to Exeter: Rafe says they will have to surrender next spring."

It was true. Everything had happened exactly as Latif had foretold. There was no food to be had for forty miles round the city. No leader had emerged; the men who should have formed an army had drifted back to their homes. The thanes threatened; they boasted of their deeds to be; but the centre of our resistance, if we were ever to fight again, would never be that noisy and disorganized camp.

"If all the Saxons had joined," I began, but Laurel put her hand on my arm. "It is harder for you, because I have Rafe; but you must not feel so alone. Surely our love, and we do love you, Wulf, is better than lying on a cold hill in Sussex?"

I smiled; I could not answer. I remembered how Rafe and I had climbed, that sunny day, up the big rocks behind Rollo's keep. I had thought (and it was true), that we had entered the playground of the gods. Happiness belongs to another air, I had wanted to say, half struggling, half at peace; but Rafe had grunted, "Breathe quietly, boy; it's a stiff pull, but there's no need to pant," and we had looked together in complete freedom into the wide sky.

"Life will change so little, Wulf; it is just these first months. You always said that you wanted to stay at Nansvean; look, you have got your wish." She smiled at me again as the young Baldur might have smiled.

I saw Rafe bowing gravely in his salt-stained clothes,

five years before. Could I ever forget Nansvean as we had walked into the courtyard, the rows of beehives showing above a low orchard wall, and the air heavy with a strange, sweet-smelling shrub? "This is a holy place," I had whispered, for we had come from many dangers; and they had all laughed. "If boys begin to talk of holiness, it is a sign they are very hungry," Laurel had teased; "Estrith, do see if you can find him something to eat."

Past happiness made it difficult. I had forgotten so much evil at the farm. "Summer will be here and harvest, and then, sooner than you believe possible, another summer," Laurel's voice pleaded. "Each one will be easier, and Rafe is lonely too, Wulf; he needs you." I smiled as she said this. It was a real sacrifice, for Laurel was terrified, I knew, that I should infect Rafe with what they called my obstinate resistance to the "new order."

"I will try to be patient," I said, lifting the jug to the barrel. It was not for Laurel, perhaps it was not for Rafe, to love freedom with that bitter, burning, all transcendent love that I felt. She took the torch from me, and I followed her up the steps with the ale. For the first time since I had landed that far-off summer day, I felt detached from the landscape, and a stranger.

"This year," Brother Thomas said, "there are seven flowers." We were sitting together on the low wall where his Breton onions had become the frilled, white trumpets of the missal angels. "When they have finished flowering, I shall dig them up and divide them. I am always afraid some donkey or a careless boy will step on them."

"I forgive you your pride," I teased him, smiling; "they

are lovelier than anything in this garden except your roses." Only I thought myself of the bedstraw and the meadowsweet.

"Wherever they came from," Brother Thomas went on, "they are English flowers now, settled here, happy here."

"Only I am not an onion." I knew what he meant.

He pushed away the weeding basket, filled with docks and small stones. "Listen, my son," he said in a grave priest's voice instead of his usual friendly tones, "it is a wretched fate to be a hostage and an exile, and you have been both, under a cruel master. People may suspect you of having been at Hastings, but they cannot prove it. You can say truthfully that you wanted to return to your northern birthplace to defend it from the Danes. It was a fault rather than a sin. Forget the marshes. Duke William is stern but he is also merciful, and we are far away from Westminster. Be wise and make your peace."

"And the price?" I asked.

"God asks no price, Wulf, only that you be penitent. The Abbot can arrange things with the Count; that is, if they even need arranging, but there must be no more foolish singing of those heathen staves." He shook his paint brush at me playfully. "No more rides to the Goon."

I looked at the frail, green stems of the trumpets, and wondered what they remembered of their home?

"Don't be foolish, my child; Rafe has made his peace."

"Rafe has more to lose than I have," I said, as gently as possible, because I knew Brother Thomas would miss me.

"I once hoped, Wulf, that those foolish fancies of yours would pass, and you would come here to join me. I would have taught you all I know of painting. But your blood is too restless for these four walls."

It was mid-April. Below us, the young grass was still too short to hide, as it did in summer, the stone cider-press that was as ancient as an altar. "Tell me," I said, breaking off a tendril of rue that was too close to the rose tree, "why do you like the Duke so much?"

"We needed regeneration, my son; we had almost become a pagan country. Duke William is a believer; he has fought the Church's enemies. Isn't it better to have him rule us than a rune-chanting drunken Earl? We have lacked a leader for twenty years; that saint, King Edward —God rest his soul—ought to have been a priest."

"Harald could not undo the damage of a generation in nine months."

Brother Thomas shivered at the mere mention of the King's name. "The Godwins, Wulf, could never have brought peace to England."

"That we shall never know," I said, scrunching the rue stem between my fingers. It was strange such glorious, dragon-fly flowers should emerge from these dull, green leaves. "Anyhow, your sailors, the men who brought you your 'onions,' will become the serfs of a Norman master whose only aim is war."

The monk stood his brushes in an earthen jar and stood up to look at his picture; it was the giant initial at the beginning of another book of prayers. "The sea, Wulf, is turbulent; it gives us food: the two-colour mackerel I painted under St. Christopher's feet at the Church, the shell-fish we eat on feast days, the samphire our poor gather in times of drought." He stooped to make playful sketches on a bit of pottery as he named them.

There was only a curve or a line, but the fish or the plant was there, more vivid than in the struggling nets. If a crab had a soul (but they said it had not, or we should not be allowed to trap it), this would be how it would look! "Only the ocean is its own master; and think of the men just our village has lost on what your poets call, I think," and he looked at me searchingly, "the whale's path." He added another curl to the samphire and handed me the sherd. "It was the way of our Saxon life when we were free; men drank, they followed heresies; oh, I know all about lighting those Midsummer fires on the Goon, it happened much too regularly to be an accident. Now we shall return to the old virtues. In the Church we shall preach the Will of God; the Duke will see such commands are obeyed. Each of us will have his place; the son will follow his father's trade; it will be as orderly as this garden. I do not allow weeds . . . ," he rooted up a little flowering daisy and flung it over the wall, "among my herbs."

"Even if the Duke is this peerless ruler," I suggested, "how do we know what his sons will be like after him? Suppose you forge us into an identical pattern; isn't it as easy to use us against order as for it?"

Brother Thomas looked troubled. His hand trembled, and he swept the curl of a petal too far into the margin. We sat in silence while he repaired the damage; then he sighed and looked up at the clear sky. "You want heaven on earth," he grumbled. "I wish you were not so stubborn-hearted; if you can't talk about pleasant things, you must not keep me from my work."

"You used to say that you could work faster when I was here to scare away the doves."

"That was last year." He looked at me sorrowfully.

"Oh, I know what you have been through; it could have brought you nearer to God, but your heart is hard and unhappy. Yes, this is Normandy now and not England, so the sooner you submit yourself the better, or . . ."

"I am not to come here again."

"Up to now I have been allowed to reason with you. I cannot say it was the Abbot's will, but I reminded him of my own battle when I painted the St. Christopher in the Church. It is just as hard as your marches, Wulf, to get a river bank to look circular on a flat wall. Even now, it is not quite right. Only if you sit here talking against the Duke, and one of the brothers hears us, how should we be able to grant you sanctuary even if you begged for it?"

So even the cloister had to bow to William's power! I said nothing, but reached over and touched the gold fringes lightly. "Why quarrel on an April morning? Have you found a name for your trumpets? They can't be onion flowers."

Brother Thomas relaxed and smiled. "A lay brother from Bodmin who has been on the Roman pilgrimage said he had seen them in the south and had heard them called narcissus. It's a Greek word, I believe. Think of God's mercy, Wulf, to have them around us here, without the perils of such a journey! When I am old this garden will be full of them. I shall live peacefully from season to season, fearing the winter less because each new spring more will be in bud. I shall sleep among them when I am too feeble to prune my trees. Where, in all the courts of Europe, will you find such treasure?"

"Nowhere," I agreed promptly, delighted at his enthusiasm; yet could he not see that if the Abbot died, a Norman bishop leagues away might direct him into a sunless cell in a distant city cloister? I hoped that the Priory could protect him, and that he would be left to live his life out here, brush in hand, absorbing the dew and light, so that these pages would flower long after last year's pippens had become withered, moss-covered stems. His garden literally excluded him from the world. Even the Normans might respect so wholehearted a devotion. It was a quality that they admired, provided that it did not run counter to their plans.

I sat on, watching him paint, not knowing how to leave. We had been so happy together, and now there was no way to make him understand the joy his companionship had given me. The herbs were beginning to sprout in the beds below; new leaves crept in slow silver along the thyme roots; a honeysuckle was climbing up the wall again. Why must discord come between us simply because we followed different masters? "How quiet it is, here, with you," I said.

"You have only to submit to the Abbot's will, my son, and you will be always welcome. All he asks you to do is to bow to the will of God."

I rose hastily, for I did not want to go with an angry word on my lips. So I was to leave Harald to bow before a Norman banner! If it were God's service, I knew where my duty lay. Harald had never ridden through helpless villages with a flaming torch to set the roofs ablaze. "It's almost noon," my fingers shot back the latch, "time I went back to the farm."

"Remember Rafe, if you will not think of yourself," Brother Thomas admonished. "I'll speak to the Abbot for you whenever you are ready. Before these trumpets are in flower next spring, you will have forgotten all about what you foolishly call submission. Come over tomorrow; I'm doing a hare, and you, with your hunting experience, can help me with the colour." He smiled at me as if I were a child who could not go to the fair and had to be comforted. "Not tomorrow," I said; "if the weather holds we shall plough." I saw him pick up his parchment as I closed the gate and hold it up to the light. Be happy, I thought, you have your pictures; I shall miss you.

This spring the path was dry. The leaves or their shadows danced over the bars of the open gate. There were cows wandering on the opposite side of the stream, and the fruit trees near the cottages were in bud. Each of us was given a choice. Whatever the Abbot might say, we were divided from the beasts because we were free to consider and select. We harvested the consequences of almost forgotten decisions, and they affected our whole world; there would be no more woodpeckers clacking harmlessly once Count Baldwin arrived here with his hawks! Choice gave us power to transform ourselves, to grow wiser; this blind obedience that they wanted was the road back to darkness.

"Master Wulf, Master Wulf!" I started. There was nobody on the path; the fields on either side were empty. There I stood foolishly, looking at a robin on a bramble until Leofric laughed and I saw him, his elbows pushing back the twigs, his jerkin and leggings so tanned by the sun it was impossible to guess their original colour, growing from the hedge more than struggling out of it. "Well, wherever have you been?" I asked, for he had not been near the farm since Christmas.

Leofric scratched his short hair and looked troubled.

"It was safer for Mistress Laurel not to come. According to the village I'm a raider."

It was so absurd that I laughed.

Leofric glanced round to make sure that we were not overheard. "I've been watching that Priory gate for an hour; I wanted to say good-bye."

"But it's too early for the fleet to sail," I said in surprise; they never left for Armorica before May.

"I'm not going on the Seagull this year; I prefer to be my own master. Do you remember what Master Latif told us? There was a place on his ship for any man unwilling to be Duke William's vassal. Once the spring gales are over he'll slip away."

"But, Leofric, you were born here in the village. I'll give you a gold piece to buy a cask of wine, and then they'll soon forget you fought for Harald. You'll be forgiven by autumn."

"There are some things, Master Wulf, that a man doesn't want to be forgiven. I've no kin and no girls to speak of, and I shall never make old bones if I stop here. One day a Norman is going to ride into the square; and if I see him either I shall lie on the stones with a smashed head or he will, and then it will be too late for me to escape. No, maybe if I sail that Inland Sea the merchant told us about, I can come home with a bag of gold when my legs are too stiff for seafaring. Only I wanted to ask you something. . . ."

"Yes?"

"After I have gone, will you tell the thane why I never came to say good-bye."

"No, Leofric," I said. "I can't tell Rafe."

He looked up at me like an unexpectedly slapped dog.

"I can't give your message, because, you see, Leofric,

I am coming with you myself. I also cannot change masters."

Leofric jumped on to the path as if he had seen a shoal of mackerel. "Sometimes I wondered if there might be two of us; and then I thought, no, Master Wulf has too much to lose."

"It's true I have much to lose," (perhaps only at this moment did I know how deep my feeling for Nansvean was), "but I'm just as much of an outlaw now as you are. When do you want to start?"

Leofric looked up at the sky. "As soon as I can get a couple of good ponies. The weather is settling and they will begin to watch the ports."

All winter I had worn a gold coin in a bag under my coat. I fancied the head on it resembled Harald so it had become a symbol of resistance to me. I unfastened my collar and jerked it out. "Will this be enough?" and added, when Leofric nodded, "then I'll be at that barn beyond the stables two nights from now."

We heard footsteps splashing up the wet bit from the stream. It was Egwin carrying a load of faggots on his shoulder. Leofric wriggled back through the hedge, gratitude and happiness on his broad muzzle of a face, though what good I was going to be to him I found it hard to imagine. "In two days," he whispered, grinned, and disappeared. A badger could not have slipped into its hole more quietly. I went to meet Egwin to throw him off the scent, but he came up, seeing nothing and grumbling as usual. "We shall pay for this sunshine," he bleated; "it's much too early." He looked at me reproachfully as if because I enjoyed it I was responsible. "Just as soon as the apple blossoms come, you'll see, there will be frost."

There is a legend that immediately before Death summons us, we regain for a day the lost peace of childhood. Before this parting, that was to me a form of death, the two days passed in momentary happiness. Later I was to think of them as part of those ocean-lost islands where the gods live, invulnerable to our fevers. At the time, they simply flashed by, without my being conscious of their passage. We fed the horses, sowed the field below the mill, simply and precisely as if we acted the drama of the rolling seasons in a temple. At night we sang the old ballads, and even Laurel smiled at them; the earliest was nearer to us now than the portents of last spring's terror.

The second day was the end of the "fish and flower" month, as the children call it, when there are more primroses than grasses in the lanes, and the fishermen try a first, short sail. I came back early with the horses and, after I had stabled them, walked up to the meadow where Laurel was feeding her chickens. It was almost sunset, a green sky tapered into straw-yellow, the everyday colours of spring. Everything was washed and clear; the thorn was flowering; white clover roamed under my feet. Laurel was sprinkling grain; she had on her new dress that was neither brown nor amber but a weave of both. As I came up, she smiled, her hair blowing in the light wind. "What a summer it is going to be, Wulf, look at the blossoms!"

It was high enough to look down on the sea, rolling between the cliffs. The waves, I thought, copied the white thorn, as they broke over the rocks. "You are happier now," Laurel said, "I am so glad."

"Yes," I answered truthfully, "the sun always makes a difference."

"I am going to tell you a secret, Wulf." For the first time in many weeks our eyes met. "Rafe wants to give you Trewoon, not to farm it for us but for your own."

Afterwards I was glad that Laurel had told me, for she must have seen, must have been able to tell Rafe what his news meant to me. "I love Trewoon," I said, "almost as much as I love you," and I touched her head, lightly and gently; it was the first time since July. She shook my hand off, but she did not move. "There is one thing you must do first."

"And that is . . ."

"You cannot live with an old crone in the kitchen to bake your bread and mend your clothes. No, Wulf, you have to find a girl."

"There will be no one after you, Laurel; you know that. You will be with me, wherever I am, always. I shall see you in the lane below the beehives where you came to us that first morning; I shall see you as you took the dog-rose from me, so brief, so soon over."

"Wulf, dear . . ."

"Trewoon is miles away, and a good farmer is shepherd to his fields as well as to his flocks," I said as lightly as I could. "We shall not meet often."

"We cannot order love to come to us," Laurel answered gently. "I could not help its being Rafe; but in time, Wulf, and don't be so obstinate," she tapped my shoulder playfully, "make us happy; find yourself a friend. Our children will be able to come over then to play with yours; there will be no real separation."

I shook my head. "Love, as you say, cannot be commanded."

The clover zigzagged across the grass; I picked up Laurel's empty pail. It seemed to me that something must happen. I had been saved from Normandy, saved from Hastings, this could not be the end. Without knowing it, I suppose, I had dreamed of returning from my voyages to end my life with Rafe and Laurel exactly as it was now. I had been too absorbed by the horror of the winter to see that they had already changed. "The wars are over," Laurel took me by the arm, "when you see the oats growing in your own fields you will say it is for the best."

"No!" I shouted, "no!" It was the battle rage, the flood that grips you in single combat, before the first axe-swing; "no, we together, Harald and England, had beauty, had power in our hands and it has been destroyed. What comes may be endured, but there is no flower in it and no fulfilment. It was a quite uncommon beauty, as if the gods came, as if they went away. . . ."

"Be patient, Wulf, what else can I do?"

Do! If Laurel had loved me we should have raced triumphantly to the coast; we should have had life, though it were only for a moment, as the heroes knew it in their mating. Leofric would have brought the row-boat to the shore, and as we waded out through the limpid, curling waves we should have been happy beyond feeling. One look now and I should understand the globe, from the recurrent cruelty of winter to that blossom in September's arch, the falling star. If she turned away, it was not simply the loss of Laurel and my love; it was all the things that I should never learn, the doom to grope unsatisfied through the years, with even the memory of our valley spoilt. I stood there feeling that she must speak, must, at this final moment, understand.

"Come, Wulf, the others are waiting; we must go." Laurel's voice was kind and troubled, but it was a surface pity, nothing more. A bough rustled, somebody shouted, there was Estrith waving to us from the yard; we turned and walked side by side, without saying a word, down the meadow to the farm.

At midnight I slipped across to the barn to wait for dawn. It was not easy to cross the yard in the intense blackness without kicking a pebble and so waking the dogs; but I moved cautiously until my fingers felt the latch. I had hidden some fleeces under the rafters on the previous day, and I drew them quickly round me for I was shivering with cold.

Time dragged. It was such a repetition of my previous escape, that I kept seeing the sandy dunes with their coarse, white shells. Only, as a boy, I had imagined that once away from Rollo's men, we should be free. How could I have known at fifteen that the world's doom and Normans, if they were part of it, were facts a generation must accept. Was it worth while for the sake of a possible illusion, one side of my brain taunted, to go off again towards a form of death? Rafe had love; Laurel, contentment; I had chosen liberty. My happiness was past, that I knew, whatever might befall. There would be moments naturally (I seemed in prescience to feel them now), but they would be calm. The deep, wild exultation of my youth was buried at Nansvean under the clover that I should never tread again, with the berries I should never taste. I had simply to open this door, clench my fists and conform to the Abbot's will; then I should have Cornish earth, Trewoon, Rafe's help and Laurel's voice. A few steps back—how they would all welcome me. Leofric would forgive me; I had given him gold, he could easily reach Latif's ship. Was it not reasonable to be fluid, to shape one's destiny with, and not against, the stream? Everybody whispered, "Go back," except Gwyneth. Her words never changed, if ever I thought of them. "Harald's homage—," she said, "loyalty laid in a lonely land." Yes, of what use were words and promises, the arrogant pennants, if we followed them merely so long as they involved no sacrifice? "It was the Earl's pride," Egwin would grunt till doom's day, with that crazy joy fools have when greatness is overthrown; "his obstinacy ruined Kent when all he had to do was to become the Duke's vassal, and nobody would have lost a pole of land." If I stayed here (I had to comfort myself in the cold and the darkness), exasperation would drive me to quarrelling; and, as Laurel's hair whitened and Rafe forgot to polish his sword, I should eat out what was left of my heart in longing for what I might have been at Micklegarth.

It was so black that no purple was visible in the hollow of the opposite wood, nor could I distinguish one pebble from the other in the yard. It was too wintry for the owls. As I shut my eyes and drew the fleeces round my shoulders again, I seemed to mount the steps of a great tower. Below me, a white-roofed city stretched towards the splendid, banner-blue crescent of the sea. I moved slowly, for I had on heavy armour; yet it was not my own, it had not shaped itself to my movement but was stiff and new. A shaft of light caught the shield rim and almost blinded me—looking down, I saw that the plates of it were gold. Then I remembered Latif's words, "Only the Varangians guard the Emperor's hall."

I saw the low, honey-coloured parapet, but it was the

sombre moors, the great stone keep, all the love and loss of my long journeys that I felt as I climbed, formed into the strict pattern of a song. Rodwen lifted up the apple branch to bind it to the wall, but the Danes had eaten the fruit. Suppose I had run away that autumn night and never sailed to Normandy? If I were a Yorkshire franklin tethered to my beeves, as the logs crackled on a peaceful fire and they brought in the ale, should I tremble because each winter was a stepping stone to death? How had Leofwen died? I came to the top step; I turned away from the balustrade, from the beautiful mosaic of distant, oblong gardens, to the deep well that was less memory than experience and whose depths narrowed till I was again the child throwing pebbles into a pool and building stories from their circles. We had missed the way; thus we had returned alive from Hastings. Motive succeeded motive till the past became as shadowy as this half-seen future, till all trembled into the garden wings of the brooch I once had dropped, held together by the dark, narrow body of this uncertain present.

I had thought to make a song for Harald, to be sung from Norway to the Faroes. I had seen myself joining a Cornish army to wrest our meadows from the Conqueror's grasp. Now I knew that these were dreams, a salve for the heart, all the treasure that I should take from England. Only I knew also that once—supreme honour for a foreign-born barbarian—I should watch over Micklegarth. What was William and our discords to my master-to-be? Fishers brawling by a foggy shore—that is how he might think of us—he, whose city was the centre of the globe, whose proudest merchants shrank against the wall for fear of touching the imperial emblem fixed to my Varangian cloak. Yes, that one evening when the sentinels turned in archaic ceremony at sunset to salute the Emperor of the East, I myself, and this was my reward, would lay my homage and my loyalty before the memory of Harald and a freedom that we alone in our cold island had conceived.

Light came slowly through the slats of the door. I shook the fleeces, rolled them up and put them where Egwin would be sure to find them. Oh, it was imagination I knew, yet as I opened the latch I seemed to see, not our quiet valley but high, snow-covered hills. It was a long journey away, perhaps as many years as I had already lived; yes, so far off that English sounded strangely in my ears and Laurel had become the same quiet memory that Rodwen was now. The path was sandy and narrow and I walked along it slowly, not reluctantly, but surprised, aware that on a crest among those mountains was my last battle and my home.

Then the cold dawn brought me to myself and I looked up at Nansvean and the first, early apple flowers above the wall. Last night, Laurel had touched my sleeve. "Sleep well, Wulf, may summer bring you happiness." No season could give me that, but it might bring change, it could give fortitude. I tried to think only of the ship as I ran across the field to join Leofric. I felt nothing; I saw nothing. I should not even have turned as we galloped off, if he had not paused "to say good-bye to the valley." There it was, under the pale sky, already detached from me, absorbed in its own dreams. What did my coming or my going matter to these ancient boulders that had been as sleepy, as indifferent, when the Romans sailed? I jerked my rein and the horses bounded forward. A weasel scurried along a bank; there was dew on the ground. Twigs snapped, a stone rolled, we turned on to the highway. The five years, from landing to leaving, were as a single July rose.